KIRSTEN KRUEGER

NERO'S DOMINION

AN AFFINITIES NOVELLA

NERO'S DOMINION: An Affinities Novella

ISBN: 978-1-7329014-7-6 paperback
ISBN: 978-1-7329014-6-9 ebook

Cover and Interior Art by: Ilona Parttimaa

AFFINITIES NOVELS

Blood

Nerve

AFFINITIES NOVELLAS

The Pixie Prince

Nero's Dominion

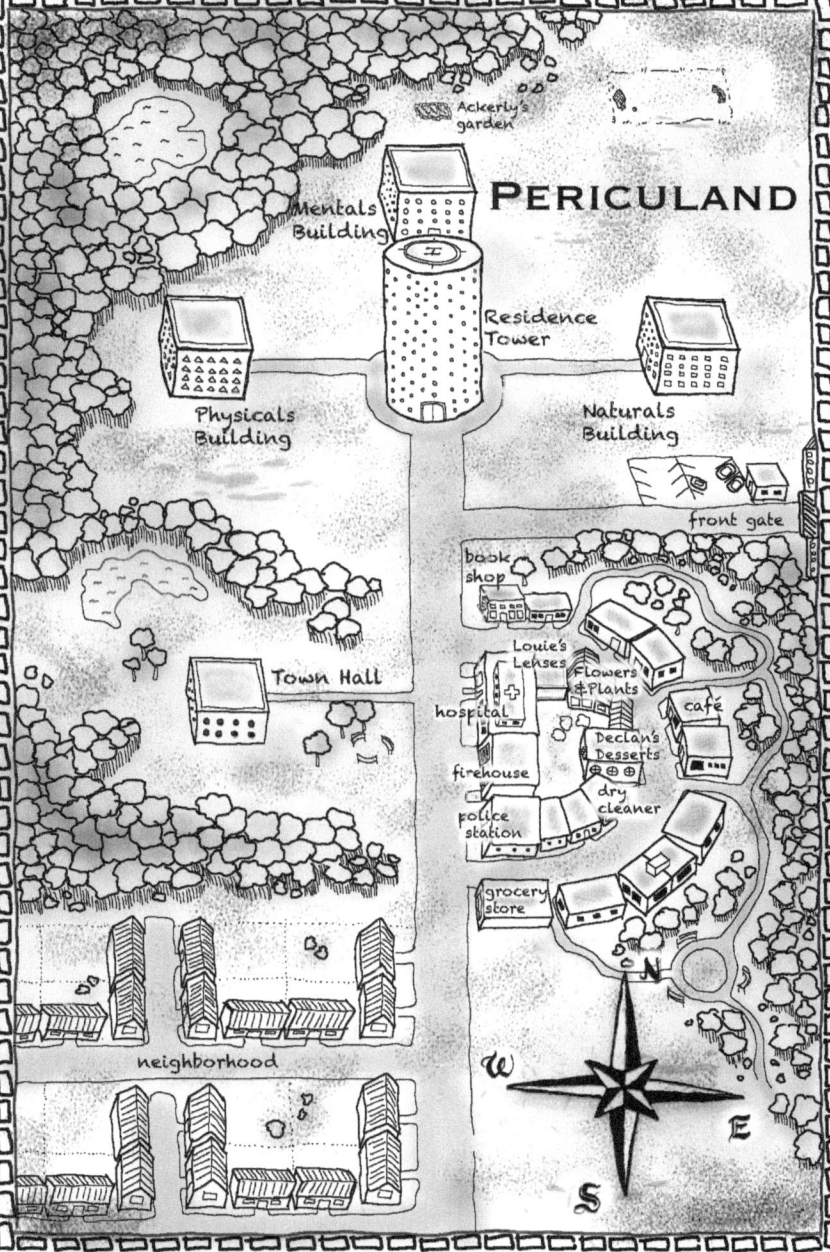

1

The Strength of Rage

Nero had been instructed not to scowl during the wedding ceremony, but obviously, not scowling wasn't an option for him. Especially when this little mouse of a kid, *Hartman*, stood directly beside him.

The day his mother had informed him she would marry Edward Corvis had been a day of elation for Adrianna Barrius and a day of rage for Nero Barrius. Even at the age of eight, the boy had expected it; as far as he knew, his mother hadn't had as much as a date until she'd met *Eddy*—or as her mother requested he call him, *Daddy*—last October. Since then the two had been attached, which meant Nero was stuck spending the majority of his time with this freckled runt.

In Nero's mother's eyes, Hartman was an angel. She'd cooed at him like he was an adorable puppy for months, and Nero ensured his disgust was apparent. He harassed the kid whenever he could, hoping Eddy would fear for his son's safety and break it off with Adrianna. Nero's mother would be distraught, of course, but her son would comfort her.

Or he would have if Eddy had succumbed to his plans. Somehow, his bullying of Hartman had failed, for their parents were marrying at this very moment. Nero would have to resort to physical violence in the future, he supposed.

There had been ample opportunity for him to hit Hartman. Even now, in the middle of the wedding, he easily could have whopped his fist into the kid's oh-so-*cute* nose. They practically stood shoulder to shoulder—although, Hartman's shoulder barely reached Nero's elbow—and the audience before them was too busy weeping over Adrianna and Edward's sentimental vows to notice.

But as much as Nero despised the Corvises, he couldn't ruin this day for his mom. If he loved one person in this world, it was her. Besides, Nero wasn't really in the mood to do a ton of chores to pay off the resulting blood damages to Hartman's over-priced outfit.

Today, the boys wore matching black suits with watermelon-pink ties—his mother's favorite color. Nero was tempted to bloody his own attire just so he wouldn't be associated with the twit stationed on his left. As requested by Adrianna, Nero and Hartman were *both* ring bearers, condemned to stand at the end of the line of groomsmen and endure the ogling and the "awes" from the spectators.

Nero would have been able to suffer through it if Hartman weren't trembling against him. He'd known since the announcement of his mother's ingenious plan that the kid would annoy the crap out of him throughout the ceremony with his constant quivering. That was why he'd initially suggested that Hartman be the flower girl instead. His mother had given him a sad face, and the matter hadn't been further discussed.

Now, Hartman's jittery nerves ignited Nero's annoyance, and he wanted nothing more than to drag him out of this ornamental church and pummel him in the parking lot. Even that probably would have been considered sacrilege, though, so maybe he'd have to haul him all the way across the street to the diner and do it there. Nero didn't really have a preference; anything to get him out of this stuffy room would have been welcomed.

"Is your dad here?" Hartman hissed, bouncing on his toes as he spoke. "I don't see him…"

"Of course you don't see him," Nero growled under his breath. "You're too short—and you don't know what he looks like, anyway. And *no*," he added when the boy's mouth flopped open again, "he's not here. He ditched my mom before I was even born. Why would he be here?"

"Well…you visit him sometimes, don't you?"

"Yeah, so? That doesn't mean he cares about my mom," Nero huffed, biting his tongue before he could add a bitter "or me." He didn't like conversing with this piglet, and he certainly didn't like conversing about his father. The mere mention of the man made him want to rip apart the church pews.

"Your dad sounds mean. I don't know why anyone wouldn't like your mom."

A surge of jealousy flared in Nero's chest, but he couldn't *blame* the kid for admiring his mom. Everyone who met Adrianna Barrius adored her; she possessed a deep kindness that Nero would never comprehend. It radiated from her, especially now as she stood at the altar holding Eddy's hands. Her dark brown hair gleamed like maple syrup, dotted with pink flowers to match the boys' ties, and her embroidered dress exuded such beauty that even Nero had to appreciate it. Though she dwarfed Eddy in height and girth, she looked like a delicate princess, beloved by all except Nero's father, *Peter Miller.*

"Yeah, he's an ass," was his response to Hartman. The little boy squeaked at the use of profanity, and Nero rolled his eyes. Such a softy, like his father. To Nero, Eddy Corvis could hardly be considered a man. He was smaller than Adrianna, scrawny and boney with childish freckles, pale blond hair, and nerdy glasses. Hartman was a miniature version of him—minus the glasses. Nero loathed them both.

There wasn't a specific reason for why he did. The Corvises had been nothing but cordial to him—but maybe that was the problem: They were *too* nice. So nice, in fact, that Nero found his mother granting them more attention than she did him. Since meeting Eddy, Nero's visits to his wretched father's house had increased from once a month to every other weekend, and he assumed the Corvises were to blame.

His growing antagonism wouldn't help the situation, but he couldn't stop himself from hating Hartman—nor could he stop himself from tormenting the kid, even if it resulted in a rift between him and his mother.

"The rings," the priest prompted, beckoning for the boys to step forward. Hartman already had his father's golden ring in his shaking fingers, but Nero halted him with a hand to the chest before he could move.

"Give it to me," the older boy commanded, holding open his other hand, which possessed his mother's glittering ring.

"But—" His wide blue eyes darted around, from the crowd to their parents and then back up to Nero. "I want to give my dad his ring."

"I'll sit on you," he threatened through gritted teeth. "I'll crack you like paper."

"P-paper doesn't crack…"

"No, but your skull will."

The kid swallowed, his body quaking with such intensity his freckles almost seemed to vibrate. There was determination in his gaze, though; he would hand his father that ring, no matter what Nero did to him in return.

He couldn't grant the worm that satisfaction. Hartman didn't deserve more "awes" from this crowd, nor affection from Nero's mother. Nero should have given both rings. Hartman should have sprinkled flowers.

"*Give it to me*," he repeated, this time lunging to snatch the ring from the boy's tiny fingers. He would have done it without effort if Hartman hadn't *disappeared*.

One moment, the kid stood before him, clutching the ring defiantly, and the next he was gone, almost as if he'd never been there at all. Paralyzed, Nero stared at the empty space, wondering if he was in a dream—or if maybe his dreams had come true. Hartman's absence was a gift he almost didn't want to question, but…how had he *vanished*?

Gasps echoed toward the cathedral ceiling. When Nero glanced at the mass of people, he expected them to gawk at the void, as well, but they didn't. Their attention was focused on the bride and groom, and as soon as Nero spun around he realized why. The slimy little pest had reappeared before the altar, right in front of his father.

Hartman seemed as baffled as the rest of the congregation to have moved at such a rapid pace, but Nero knew the kid hadn't moved or run or even sprinted. He'd teleported.

"H-here, Dad," Hartman stuttered as he presented the ring like some holy object. Eddy still appeared horror-stricken, Adrianna looked ready to faint, the crowd murmured about the impossibility of it all—and Nero couldn't watch anymore. He didn't care that Hartman had engaged in a supernatural act, but he did care that everyone would now fawn over the kid for it.

Stomping across the platform, Nero shoved his body next to Hartman's and thrust his mother's ring in her face, disregarding that she continued gaping at the runt and ignored her son's presence completely.

"Here, Mother," Nero boomed in a voice that cut through the worried whispers. "Your ring. I hope you have a nice marriage. I—love you."

The last words were practically a gag. He hated uttering them, not because they weren't true but because they sounded…weak. Pathetic. Needy. They accomplished the purpose for which he'd spoken them, though; the simple statement tore his mother from her trance and hushed the spectators. An uneasy gleam still consumed the priest's gaze, but after the bride and groom exchanged a smile, he resumed the ceremony, acting as though nothing odd had occurred.

To Nero's delight, the rest of the wedding was rushed, and everyone soon forgot about Hartman's teleportation once they arrived at the reception venue. After a few drinks, people began joking about how absurd it was that they'd thought the boy had magically jumped from one place to another. It must have been a trick on the eyes, they claimed, and then commended Hartman for his speed and encouraged him to try out for the track team. Even Adrianna and Eddy had settled into this ignorant state of denial, laughing along with their family and friends.

Nero didn't laugh; he didn't even crack a smile throughout the entire celebration. Because what everyone had failed to acknowledge was that Hartman Corvis had a strange hint of orange to his blond hair now—and to his blue eyes, as well.

Something had changed within him, and while everyone was busy pretending it had never happened, Nero plotted how he could ensure it happened again. Fear seemed to drive the need for Hartman's teleportation, as exhibited during the ceremony, which meant Nero would get the chance to engage in the violence he craved—only now it would have a justifiable purpose.

Nero was, quite literally, a bastard.

Although his mother had married that asshole Corvis, she had not married Nero's father, and it was really a miracle she'd been able to pinpoint the man at all—a miracle for *her*, anyway. For Nero, it was a curse.

Peter Miller was the definition of a jerk. He'd lied to Adrianna, claiming he was single when he'd actually been *married*. It broke her heart, and Nero loathed Miller for it. His mother still wanted him to have a *relationship* with his real father, however, so every other weekend of his childhood, Nero had been subjected to spending two whole days at his father's house in western Ohio.

There wasn't a time when Nero could remember not hating the visits. Instead of being pampered by his doting mother, he was forced to perform grueling chores for his father, which included yard work and handy work. All by himself. Starting at the age of five.

He'd barely been old enough to reach the handles of the lawn mower, but he'd had to push it up and down his father's long stretch of land. He'd barely been strong enough to pick up the hammer, but he'd had to use it to fix and build various objects—and then apply his own band-aids when he accidentally nicked his fingers. All while Miller lounged inside his house, spending time with his *real* wife and his *real* kids.

The number of half-siblings Nero had was a mystery to him since he'd never actually been allowed to *meet* them. His father always insisted Nero sleep outside in a tent rather than inside the house. It would *toughen him up*, Miller said, and for a few years Nero had actually believed him. He'd always *wanted* to be tough. Without a father figure in the house, he'd felt the need to protect his mother—to be strong mentally and physically when she couldn't be. That was why he'd always done the work his father had forced on him without complaint.

By the age of twelve, the reality of his situation had begun to settle in. Miller didn't want to *toughen him up*; Miller wanted to *get rid of him*. Miller wasn't proud of Nero when he accomplished a project or spent cold nights in the heatless tent; he was simply grateful for the free labor—and the hilarity Nero's suffering brought his *real* children.

No, he hadn't met his half-siblings, but he'd seen them. They never came outside to greet him, but they watched from the windows like little rabbits, giggling to themselves whenever Nero cut his arm or stubbed his toe. He never deigned to shoot them crude gestures or yell obscenities, but he was often tempted.

Hartman was the one who received the brunt of his bloodlust, and although catching the kid had actually become a challenge, it satiated Nero's hunger for violence. Over the past four years, the teleporter's abilities had flourished, allowing him to jump from one place to the next whenever he chose. There were holes in his power, though. He could only teleport a few feet from where he began, and he had yet to teleport beyond whatever structure he was encased in. The day Nero had learned that, he'd found a trunk in their garage and locked the kid inside. He'd screamed and cried for hours before their parents heard him. Nero hadn't minded being grounded for that. It meant one less weekend at his father's, which was more of a blessing than a punishment.

Along with the slight, almost pathetic advancement of his *superpower*, Hartman's blond hair and blue eyes had morphed into a putrid, citrusy orange. Their parents had tried to be encouraging about the change, but Nero knew they were worried. Over the past few years, a group of terrorists had risen in the United States, a group of people who all had crazily colored hair and eyes—and claimed to have super-powers. Even though Hartman was only ten, their parents feared the authorities would connect him to this group's evil deeds.

Contrarily, Nero waited anxiously for the day the government knocked on their door and locked the kid in handcuffs. It would be his pleasure to advise them to place the dangerous child in a sealed box—preferably one without air.

These fantasies played in Nero's head while he mowed his father's lawn on a breezy May afternoon. The notion of Hartman in jail brightened his mood when it would have otherwise been soured by the nasty little rabbits perched beyond the glass doors at the rear of the Millers' house.

His half-family lived in a posh neighborhood, much nicer than Eddy freaking Corvis would ever afford. Their house wasn't a mansion, but it certainly could have fit Nero for a few nights a month, if only Peter allowed it. In most ways, though, he preferred his mother's home—not just because she treated him better, but because it was…unique. Adrianna and Eddy's house was a small red ranch in the woods, where they raised chickens and grew vegetables. Peter's house was a two-story suburban home identical to the rest of the neighborhood, with a perfectly flat yard that was in-distinguishable from any of the others.

It solidified the Millers as ordinary and normal—inconsequential in Nero's eyes. They weren't special; they were exactly like everyone else. Nero wanted to be better than everyone else—and he especially wanted to be better than his father.

"You missed a few spots," the man said as he sauntered through the same glass doors his kids had used to spy on Nero a few moments prior. The boy had finished mowing and was wheeling the machine back into the shed when his father's voice halted his movements. Containing a growl, he spun around to meet the man's pompous gaze.

There wasn't a hint of Nero in Peter Miller's appearance—except for the tallness, perhaps. At the age of twelve, Nero had surpassed all the kids at school and even some of his teachers. Miller, too, was abnormally tall, towering at six and a half feet. Since his mother was a tall woman, as well, Nero hoped to surpass his father one day. And then crush him like an ant.

"You should be a professional by now," Miller chided, narrowing his vibrant green eyes at the equally green grass. They were too bright for his personality, and Nero was glad he'd inherited his mother's dark features instead. "But look at this mess—patches missed everywhere, uneven lines… It's unacceptable."

Nero's jaw clenched as he followed his father's vision to these *unacceptable* spots. The few blades of grass peeking above the rest would have been impossible to detect if Nero hadn't left them there intentionally. He *had* become quite the professional at mowing the lawn, so professional that he could purposely mess up to make his father's yard look a little less perfect than the rest. It was doubtful any neighbors would notice, but Miller did, and that was all Nero cared about.

"If I'm so bad, why don't you do it yourself?" the boy huffed, finally voicing the words that had always caught in this throat. Something about today really *irked* him. Maybe it was his stupid half-siblings, still peering through the back door. Or maybe it was his father's stupid baseball cap, the one he constantly wore to taunt Nero since he wasn't allowed to wear one while he worked. Or maybe it was stupid Hartman, mocking him from afar with the fact that their parents had taken him to the amusement park today and they never, ever did that when Nero was around.

"Because I have a job—responsibilities," Miller retorted. "Your mother spoils you—she doesn't give you duties or punishments or *purpose*. You'll thank me in a few years for the work ethic I've given you."

It was true: Adrianna had never given Nero any chores. But she *had* punished him; she was punishing him right now.

"What about your other kids? Why don't they do any work?" Nero jerked his chin toward the house. A few small figures moved within, but he couldn't count how many. Were any of them bastards? Nero hoped not. He liked being different. Plus, if any of them were bastards but didn't receive the same hellish *duties*, he would murder someone.

"They have their own tasks to attend to inside," Miller assured him breezily. "Everyone possesses a different skillset, Nero, and yours is…physical. To put it kindly, you have brawn and the other children have brains. Both have different functions—"

"Are you calling me *dumb*?" He released his grip on the lawn mower to step closer to his father. The way Miller's expression flickered with apprehension made Nero's heart flutter with delight.

Still, there was slyness to the man's tone when he said, "Well, you are your mother's son."

The insult took a moment to settle, but once he processed his father's insinuation—and the lack of remorse he now displayed in its aftermath—a chasm of detestation cracked in Nero's chest, so intense his vision blurred. Sure, his mother had flaws, but this asswipe wasn't allowed to point them out and act like he was *superior*.

Miller was a tall man, but he was skinny, and even as a pre-teen Nero outweighed him in muscle. Pummeling him would be easy—and unsatisfying. What would really be satisfying, and what he'd waited years for, lay beyond those pesky glass doors.

"Well," Nero spat, hands already balled into fists at his sides, "if I'm as *dumb* as my mother, then your *real* kids must deserve a beating as much as their father."

Ah, there was the remorse. No, not remorse: *dread*. Miller didn't feel bad about what he'd said; he only feared what his bastard son would do to his precious children. Well, he certainly had need to fear, because Nero's brain had gone primal, and he'd picked his prey.

"Nero," Miller pleaded, grabbing at his arm, but the boy shoved off his attempted obstruction and stalked toward the house undeterred. He'd known for months now, maybe even years, that he was like Hartman—that he had a superpower. His jet black hair harbored a gray tint, and his brown eyes had turned ashy. There was *some* kind of ability dwelling within him, and as soon as he punched through the glass door, he knew exactly what it was: super strength.

As shards rained into the house, provoking screams and

cries, Nero's chest swelled with excitement, and he closed his eyes to focus on the power flowing through his muscles. He felt *strong*—otherworldly strong—and soon these little rats would feel another world of pain.

When his eyes flew open, all he saw was movement bathed in red. There was no calm, no coherency to this state of anger. The first thing that moved, he grabbed, and he didn't pause to think about who it was before he attacked.

Shouts slammed his ears as his fists slammed a face. The child could have been a girl or a boy, younger or older—Nero didn't know. All he knew was that hurting his half-siblings would bring Peter Miller agony, and that was all he really wanted.

Another kid tried to intervene by tugging on Nero's arm, but his fist met their nose in an instant. A third kid descended on his back, but he bucked them off like a bull. These half-siblings really were everywhere, swarming him like a horde of demonic bunnies. Nero was strong enough to fend them off, but their numbers prevented him from inflicting any more damage.

"*Enough*," Miller commanded, yanking Nero off the child he'd apparently tackled to the ground. In his haze of red, he saw nothing more than a bloody face and long hair. That he'd clobbered who he assumed to be a little girl should have disturbed him, but it didn't. He felt oddly immune to the sympathy and guilt that should have been present. After seven years of being an obedient bastard, he'd finally scratched the itch for violence, and he felt *good*.

Despite that, he needed to flee this place. His ears rang with the children's incessant yelling, the new wave of scolding from Miller, and the unnatural pace his blood flow had increased to. Without glancing back at the injuries he'd inflicted, Nero staggered over the shattered glass and out the empty doorway.

Just in time to bump into a semi-circle of cops that had formed in the backyard.

2

A Caged Animal

"So, what'd you do to land yourself in here?" the security officer asked as he guided Nero through the white-tiled halls of the juvenile detention facility. Bright blue doors lined either side, and Nero made sure he scowled at every single one. He wanted the other inmates to feel the weight of his presence before they even saw him. At his father's house, he'd allowed himself to be the subordinate, but after pummeling his half-siblings earlier that day, he'd decided he would be servile no longer. Wherever he went he'd become the alpha, and anyone who dared challenge him would pay.

"You don't know?" Nero grunted with a brief glance in the man's direction. His hair and eyes were the same shade of aged gray, but there was barely a wrinkle on his face. It was this, accompanied by the slight jostling of the metal handles on every door they passed, that convinced Nero something was off about this man.

"Nah, I'm just the security," the officer—*Charlie*, as denoted by his little name-tag—said as he casually flipped a coin in his hand. The metal snapped back toward his palm with too much swiftness for it to be a natural descent. Nero was disturbed enough to resume his door-scowling. "I never get the details—unless I'm nosy, that is."

"I've got nothing to hide. I want everyone here to know what I did—and that I'll do it again if I'm provoked." Nero paused dramatically, reveling in the curiosity written on the officer's face. "I beat up my half-siblings."

Charlie's lips twitched into a frown as he returned his attention to his coin. "That's lame—and typical. I bet over half the kids here have engaged in some domestic violence— and many of them used methods much more sadistic than a petty beating."

"*Petty?*"

"Sorry, kid," Charlie added with a wince. "You look tough and all, but…you're not the biggest fish in this pond. You're what, fifteen?"

"Twelve."

Charlie stumbled but then corrected himself. "Damn, you are oversized. All right, so maybe *one day* you'll be the big guy here, but right now there are definitely worse. Let's take your new roommate for example—he's a little guy, and I mean *tiny*, but…" The man peeked around the empty corridor for listening ears before whispering, "he killed his *mom*. His own freaking mother. I have no idea how he did it, but he did, and that runt scares the shit out of me."

Tiny and *runt* didn't make his new roommate seem threatening, but…*murdering his own mother?* Nero was definitely apprehensive as they neared the end of the hall. He could never imagine laying a finger on his mom. Even getting himself locked up here, separated from her, nibbled at his conscience. To physically harm her would have been a crime for which he'd never acquit himself.

"Why are you putting me in a cell with a *murderer?*" Nero demanded, hoping the fear didn't bleed into his tone.

"Well, he claims he didn't *mean* to murder—" Charlie's

voice came to a halt when the last doorway on the left came into view and they found it open. Pocketing his coin, the officer cautiously approached the threshold, hand on the stun-gun at his side. Nero followed at his heels and stopped once his eyes landed on the two figures within the room.

Closest to the open doorway stood a man in a peculiarly wine-colored suit. His lips curved into a simper at the sight of the boy and the officer, but Nero barely noticed the change in expression. All of his focus was locked on the long hair framing the man's face, a shade of pink that belonged beneath one's skin, not atop one's head. It was an even deeper hue than his lips—but the same exact hue as his irises.

Was he one of the superhuman terrorists Nero had seen on the news? If he was, then Charlie probably was, as well, because the security officer's posture had relaxed as if this man's oddly-colored hair made him *less* suspicious.

"Visitors aren't permitted in this area," Charlie said slowly.

"I apologize," the man replied with a respectful bow of his head. The gesture should have made him seem weak and submissive, but Nero still felt a tinge of disquiet, maybe even more now than he had before. "They've banned Hastings from the visitor's section, so I figured this was the only way I'd be allowed to see him."

It wasn't until the man gestured toward the boy slumped on his bed that Nero really looked at him. Deep auburn hair hung in strands around his face, obscuring half his features from view. His skin had naturally tanned undertones, but it seemed considerably dulled, as if he hadn't seen the sun in years. What really struck Nero was this boy's *size*. He was indeed a runt, as small as stupid little Hartman. His limbs were less than half the width of Nero's, and the thought of this kid *murdering* someone—he actually barked a laugh.

The boy's head snapped up at the sound, his hair shifting enough for his eyes to peek through. Nero froze immediately, the chuckles dying on his tongue. This boy's eyes were *red*—blood red.

"I assume you're Hastings's new roommate?" the pink-haired man inquired, that creepy smile still plastered on his lips. "I'm glad he'll finally have one. The poor boy must become lonely."

"Is he your son?" Nero coughed out.

The man's expression darkened, but his voice remained cool as he said, "He's more of an *interest* of mine. It's unlikely you've heard, but I'm in the process of building a town for… people like us. Perhaps…" The man paused, scrutinizing Nero with keen eyes. "Perhaps people like you, too."

Nero wasn't sure what to make of that. He knew "people like us" was probably a reference to their weird matching hair and eyes, but he wasn't like that. He'd always had dark hair and eyes, and that wasn't abnormal…was it?

Uncharacteristically curious, he actually planned to ask the man to elaborate, but then Charlie spoke again, all apprehension forgone as his jaw hung open.

"You're—Mr. Periculy," the officer spluttered, instantly dipping his head. Nero saw the difference in this gesture—the respect, the *fear*—and realized Mr. Periculy's bow hadn't been submissive at all; it had been one of authority and intimidation. "I-I didn't know—"

"No worries, Mr. Campbell," the man said with a cordial tone. Nero heard it for what it was, though: a mockery—a way to demean this officer by implying that although Charlie had been ignorant, Mr. Periculy was not. "Is this your son?" he prompted, glancing between the gray-haired man and Nero with intrigue. "The resemblance is uncanny."

"N-no. I wouldn't be allowed to escort my own son into prison."

"Of course not," Mr. Periculy answered, but he wasn't looking at Charlie anymore; he was staring at Nero. "What's your name?"

Puffing up his chest, he proclaimed, "Nero Barrius."

"No," Charlie contradicted, his voice firmer now. "You're Nero Corvis. That's what your papers said, at least."

Heat crept into his cheeks at Charlie's words, at Mr. Periculy's stare. It wasn't anger, though; it was embarrassment. These men didn't know the Corvises, but it still shamed Nero that they now knew he was related to them. The Corvises were pathetic excuses for men, but Barrius—Barrius was a strong name. It reflected the resilience he and his mother possessed. Even if Adrianna had changed their names legally, they would always be Barriuses. He would never settle for *Corvis*.

"Regardless of your name," Mr. Periculy began carefully, "I do hope to see you in the future, Nero."

"I'll ensure you can return here to visit, Mr. Periculy," Charlie gushed with enough smarminess to make Nero roll his eyes. "Anything you need around here, you just ask for Charlie."

"Will do, Mr. Campbell." The man's face flashed with a patronizing gleam before he nodded to Hastings and exited the room.

"I'll escort you!" Charlie called as he dashed to follow him into the hall. Nero was severely disappointed when the officer, in his haste, took a moment to close and bolt the door from the outside.

"Asshole," he muttered as he surveyed the tiny room he would share with this tiny boy. Nero was tempted to grab any one of the desks, stools, or bunks and hurl it at the concrete. He wished he had the strength to smash the walls, but all he could do was beat up children, and even his miniature roommate had accomplished more than that.

"Hastings, huh?" was all Nero could think to say to the kid, if he could even call him a *kid*. Hastings was definitely younger, but he radiated a strange sense of maturity—a calmness that most children, like Hartman, couldn't master. "Where'd you get a name like that?"

"Where'd you get a name like Nero?" the boy asked, his voice unexpectedly eerie and defiant.

"It's the name of a Roman Emperor."

"A tyrannical emperor who was overthrown and couldn't even manage to commit his own suicide."

Nero opened his mouth to retort but then clamped it shut. "I don't like history," he decided after a few seconds of contemplation. "Let's talk about that Periculy guy instead. What's his deal?"

Hastings's off-white prison shirt shifted on his bony shoulders as he shrugged. "He visits me."

"Yeah, I gathered that. *Why?*"

Red eyes fixing on the ground, he sighed. "I'm his experiment."

"What…kind of experiment?"

Hastings met his gaze, but he didn't open his mouth again. Instead, he swung his legs onto the bed and rested his head on the pillow, closing those burgundy eyes off from the world. It *was* late. Nero had spent the entire day at the police station by his father's house, listening through the walls as his half-siblings moaned about their deserved beating. There had been enough witnesses to throw Nero directly into juvie. He would have a trial in a few weeks, but he would lose. This cell would be his home, and this freak would be his roommate.

The entire prospect was tiring enough that Nero also wanted to flop back on his bunk and sleep forever. He wasn't sure how he felt about sleeping in the same room as this stranger, though—this mother-murderer. Nothing had ever frightened Nero, but Hastings did. Especially when he awoke the next morning with purple bruises sprouting on his arms.

"Is it weird that I miss Nero?" Hartman whispered as he, his dad, and his stepmom entered the detention center's visitation room. The walls were so *white*, just like his dad's shirt. Adrianna wore watermelon pink today, as always—but she didn't like to be called *Adrianna*. Since the wedding, his stepmom had insisted to be called Mom, as if she were his real mother.

Hartman wasn't sure he liked that.

Well, no—he did like *her*, but he didn't like the idea of her replacing his real mom. His dead mom.

Expectantly, Hartman looked up at his dad.

"It is a little weird," the man agreed quietly. His blue eyes were fixed worriedly on the room before them. Hartman's irises had been the same powdery blue once. Now they were an unnatural orange, and it made him even more nervous than he'd always been. Even at the age of ten he knew he wasn't normal, and in a way, it did make him miss Nero. No one at school liked him, and Nero hadn't either, but at least his stepbrother had given him some attention. To Hartman, they'd been friends, and so, for the past three months, he'd been friendless.

"Is it weird that I wish he could come home and lock me

in the trunk in the garage?" Hartman pressed. His father gave him a wince, since anything they said would echo off the empty walls. The door had shut behind them, and they approached the center of the room, where prisoners and their families sat at wooden tables.

The first who caught Hartman's attention was a boy with pear-green eyes...and hair. He wasn't particularly large or intimidating, but he *was* staring at Hartman in an unsettling way. As soon as he acknowledged this in his mind, the strange boy *smiled*, and it wasn't a pleasant smile; it was creepy, widening with the expanse of Hartman's unease.

"*Nero*," Adrianna gushed, drawing him back to his family. They'd reached the closest table now, where Nero sat. Not much had changed about him over the past three months; he was still massive, still grumpy, and judging by the way his eyes narrowed, he still hated Hartman.

There was something different about his eyes, though. They weren't the same coffee brown as Adrianna's anymore. They were gray, like two sharp rocks—like his *hair*.

"Nice hair," Hartman said before he could stop himself. Nero's lips curled over his teeth in a snarl, and his fists clenched atop the table. That was when Hartman realized he was *handcuffed* to the table. His amusement was difficult to hide.

"Nero," Adrianna repeated, taking the empty seat directly across from her son's. Hartman's dad assumed the one beside her, meaning Hartman was stuck with the chair farthest from Nero—and closest to the weird green-haired boy, who continued studying him even as the kid's parents talked to him in hushed tones.

"How have you been?" Adrianna inquired, pulling Hartman's gaze away from the other prisoner. "Are they treating you well here?"

"I'm used to being mistreated." Nero cocked his head accusingly, referring not to his mother but his father. Over the years, Hartman had picked up on the subtle hints his stepbrother had voiced implying his father wasn't a nice man.

Even now, Adrianna dismissed it. Reaching across the table, she took her son's hands and looked earnestly into his granite gray eyes. "I'm so happy we're finally together ag—"

Nero jerked his hands away from her, but he couldn't remove them from the table, so he resorted to keeping them on the very edge, balled into fists. "Why are you here?" he demanded, shooting a circumspect glance at the other delinquents in the room. "To scold me for what I did?"

"Of course not," Adrianna soothed. Her hands twitched like she wanted to reach for his again, but she didn't. "I've just missed you."

"Me too," Hartman piped up—and then immediately regretted it when Nero growled. "I-I kept your caterpillar alive for you. It…turned into a butterfly a few weeks ago."

"You mean that stupid little insect you tried to put in my room? I should have murdered that thing before I left."

"Before you were taken away, you mean," Hartman began, but when Nero lunged forward, he hastily amended, "Yeah—yeah, you left. And, um…it wouldn't have mattered if you murdered it, anyway. As soon as I let it free in the yard a bird swooped down and ate it."

"Good," the older boy grunted, relaxing into his chair. "Did you cry?"

Hartman looked down at the lines in the wooden table and mumbled, "Not that much…"

With a snort, Nero looked to his mother. "You should be grateful I didn't end up like this little baby. He wouldn't last one day in this place."

"I'm…glad you're doing well," Adrianna managed.

"Have you made any friends?" Hartman's dad asked with a weak smile. It was far less encouraging than the one he gave Hartman whenever he posed this same question.

"*No*, and I don't plan to. I'll be done with this shit-fest any day."

Meeting her husband's eyes from the corners of hers, Adrianna carefully said, "Where did you learn that word, sweetie?"

"What, *shit?* Not sure, probably from good old Miller. He'd always tell me I did a 'shitty job' on this or 'shitty work' on that. One time he called me a *'piece* of shit.' Don't look so surprised, *Mother.* You slept with the asshole. Bet he said much dirtier things to—"

For some reason, Hartman's body chose that exact moment to sneeze. He thought it was a blessing, a nice interruption to what had the potential for an unpleasant turn of conversation, until the sneeze caused him to *move*.

It was teleportation. He knew that was what it was, but he hated to admit it. Not because it wasn't cool—it was *badass*, a word his father would gasp to hear come from his mouth. The problem was that *he* wasn't badass. He was…sort of… pathetic. Yeah, he had teleportation abilities, but he lacked the skills, which was very clearly portrayed when his sneeze involuntarily shot him a measly six inches to the side, enough to shift him off his chair, which then allowed him to collapse to the tiled floor.

The roar of Nero's laughter cut through the air. When Hartman finally righted himself and climbed back into his seat, his stepbrother was still chortling. The mirth was so malicious that, for the first time, Adrianna appeared genuinely disturbed by her son.

"*Nero,*" she hissed with enough aggression to actually shut him up. She shot Hartman a pleading look; he wasn't supposed to teleport in public. Unfortunately, it was rarely his decision. Adrianna knew this, as did his father, so neither of them scolded him before Nero's mother continued, "Your attitude is…darker, honey. Is everything okay?"

Hartman didn't think dark*er* was correct. Nero had always been this dark; he just hadn't fully shown it. Now, in this atmosphere, where deviance was the norm and cruelty was expected, his true colors—or lack of color—seeped past the surface.

"It's fine…" he grumbled, eyes drifting to his left, where the green-haired boy sat with his family. Hartman was almost afraid to look again, but his curiosity won. This time, the boy wasn't simply smiling; he was jumping his eyebrows at Nero *tauntingly.*

Hartman knew exactly what taunting Nero earned a person. Apparently this boy did, too, because as he studied him closer now, Hartman saw a huge bruise on the kid's jaw. In a place like this, it could have been inflicted by anyone, but based on the animosity wafting off his stepbrother, it must have been a Nero-induced injury.

"Well…" Adrianna started, straining to peek at her son, "if you say it's fine, this might be a good time to tell you the court's decided to extend your sentence here."

At that, Nero's head whipped back toward her. A vein bulged in his neck, and Hartman instinctively shrunk lower in his chair. "*Why?*"

"You've been deemed a…domestic threat. And I think…" She trailed off when her eyes finally lifted and caught onto the green head of hair at the next table. Apprehension morphed her features as she breathed, "Nero, they haven't found out about your...condition, have they?"

His condition. Like Hartman's condition. Like the green-haired boy's condition. Since Nero's *incident* with his half-siblings, his mom and Hartman's dad had whispered about the possibility that he, too, suffered from the same predicament as the superpower-wielding terrorists. Adrianna was in denial about it, but Hartman was certain his stepbrother's ability had something to do with an uncanny amount of strength.

"No, Mom," Nero muttered, casting a glare at the green-haired boy. What ability might *he* possess—supernatural creepiness?

Even though Nero was in one of his classically testy moods, Hartman couldn't prohibit himself from asking, "Do you know that kid?"

"Yeah, and I hate him almost as much as I hate you. He and my roommate..."

"Bully you?" Hartman suggested when Nero didn't finish.

"*Irritate* the *shit* out of me," he corrected with pointed scowls at each of his family members.

"Is that...why he has that bruise?"

With an eerily dazzling grin, Nero said, "I'm glad you recognize my work."

"Tell them about *your* bruises, Corvis."

All four Corvises pivoted toward the green-haired boy. Based on his sly smirk in Nero's direction, it was clear whom he had addressed.

"*You little—*"

"What bruises, Nero?" Panicked, Adrianna reached across the table again and pushed up the sleeves on his pale gray prison attire, exposing his meaty forearms—which were riddled with contusions. They ranged from tiny, pea-sized dots to masses so deeply purple that it looked like someone had tried to paint planets on his skin.

With a sharp gasp, Adrianna gawked at the bruises. "Who did this to you? Was it *him?*" Her gaze flew to the green-haired boy, whose expression was smug enough to incriminate him.

Nero shook his head, ripping his arms from her grasp. "*No.* It was...my roommate."

"Your roommate's been...abusing you?"

"And you've been *letting* him?" Hartman chimed in.

"No, I haven't been *letting* him. If you keep talking, though, I'm gonna *let* my fist break your—"

"This is unacceptable," Adrianna insisted. "We can't allow this kind of corruption!"

"*Calm down.*" Nero tugged down his sleeves, brow furrowing into an odd expression almost like *embarrassment.* "It doesn't matter. I told you, I'm *fine.*"

"No, you're not, Nero." His mother hiccuped. Then she bit her lip—a gesture Hartman had learned meant she was suppressing tears. It had become so common over the past few months of Nero's absence. Now even his presence seemed to make her sad. And that made Hartman's dad sad. Which made Hartman sad, as well.

"*Stop,*" Nero demanded, eyes darting around as the rate of his mother's hiccups heightened.

"More concerned about your reputation than your own mother, Corvis?" the green-haired boy crooned.

Nero's reaction to the challenge happened so rapidly Hartman would've missed it if he'd blinked. One moment, his stepbrother was seated in his chair, grinding his teeth, and the next, he'd lurched up, yanking the table by the chains connecting it to his wrists.

Adrianna screamed as the table flew above them, and Hartman's dad scrambled to pull them out of its range. Hartman didn't need help, though; before his brain could comprehend what was about to unfold, his body teleported him. A whole *three feet*.

Even at such a profoundly far distance, Hartman felt the *whoosh* of air when the wooden table descended to the floor. It shattered, blasting debris in all directions. He covered his eyes with his arm, but that didn't shield his ears from the shouts of horror. When he finally did look upon the scene, every person ogled in their direction, not just at Nero but at Hartman, too.

"He just *teleported!*" a woman cried, but her words were soon forgotten, because from where he'd knelt among the shards of wood, Nero finally extended to his feet, no longer chained to the table. The handcuffs hung limply from his wrists, now more like weapons than constraints.

"*Don't,*" Adrianna seethed before he could take a step toward the green-haired boy. Tears flowed down her blotchy cheeks, and she stomped over the wreckage toward her son without fear.

The rest of the room brimmed with terror. Many visiting families had already scurried toward the exit, and the remaining juvenile prisoners, chained to their own tables, cowered as low as they could. All except the green-haired weirdo, of course. His bright eyes scanned the entire Corvis family as if he could read them like a book.

"Do you know why we came here today, Nero?" Adrianna whispered. Sorrow simmered in her eyes as she met her son's. "We wanted to determine if you were stable enough to bring home. Your sentence could be over in a few weeks—if we could attest to your good nature. But I can't anymore…nor do I want to. What will you do to Hartman if you come home?"

Nero's nose wrinkled. "It's always about that little *shit*, isn't it?"

At the angle he stood, he was blind to the three guards creeping behind him. Adrianna saw them, and Hartman could tell by her rigid posture that she knew this was goodbye to her son—for now, at least. "I'm sorry, Nero," she said before the guards seized his arms.

He bucked to fight them off, but one had a stun-gun, and he crumbled at its blow. They were upon him then, and Adrianna was upon Hartman and his dad, ushering them out as quickly as possible. Even in the rush, Hartman took a second to peek over his shoulder. The strange boy who had instigated this entire scene watched Nero with the slightest hint of remorse. As soon as the brute elbowed one of the guards in the nose, that remorse dissipated, replaced with a deep loathing. It scared Hartman more than Nero's rage.

"So…we're not bringing Nero home?" Hartman asked once they'd safely exited the detention center. The sky was much too blue to reflect their gloom.

"No, son," his father replied since Adrianna shook too profusely to speak. "Not now."

Hartman was young and naive, but he knew well enough what usually accompanied a "not now."

Not ever.

3

Wildlife Transportation

Nero was idly breaking his plastic fork into tiny pieces when the officers stomped into the cafeteria to summon him.

It was an ordinary Sunday afternoon, marked by the luxurious, rock-hard pizza they were only gifted on holy days. Physically fragile kids like that green-haired freak, Albie, probably broke teeth on it. Not Nero—he ate his slice in three chomps, then waited patiently for others to trudge over and gift him with theirs.

Many did. Although he sat utterly alone at every meal, Nero had gained everyone's respect in juvie. Kids knew how to fall in his good graces, and some, like Albie, willingly chose to remain on his bad side. Maybe not all of the boy's broken teeth were from the pizza.

Over three years had passed since Nero had been condemned to this detention center. As far as he was aware, his sentence would never end. What he'd done hadn't even been *that* bad, but the government didn't care about what he'd done. They feared what he might do with his *ability*. So they kept him locked in this cage like an animal they didn't have the patience to train.

Not even his own mother possessed the dedication to

tame him. Yeah, she'd visited throughout the years, and she often brought that twitchy little carrot-head with her, but she never talked about the possibility of his homecoming.

The worst part was he couldn't manage to loathe her for the neglect. He still ached to see her; still felt a tingle of excitement whenever that officer, Charlie, told him she'd arrived; still...loved her. She was the only person he'd ever loved—maybe the only person he ever *could* love.

His feelings frustrated him to the point of aggression— aggression he often unleashed on Albie, or whichever unfortunate inmate happened to be within the vicinity. In Nero's mind, the green-haired boy was half the cause for his mother's absence. If he hadn't provoked Nero during the visitation all those years ago, his mother surely would have fought for his freedom; his continued incarceration had nothing to do with his hot-headedness at all.

So he pummeled Albie whenever an opportunity arose. He didn't let any of the other violent kids lay a finger on him, though. If Albie received a beating, it would be by Nero's hands. He'd made that clear more than once.

Likewise, Hastings had made it clear that if anyone injured Albie, they would pay a price. It wasn't uncommon for Nero to wake the morning after giving Albie a black eye with his own bruises he didn't remember acquiring. His mother demanding they move Nero to another room hadn't yielded the desired result, nor had it stopped Hastings from practicing his demonic talent.

At this very moment, Nero wouldn't have been surprised if contusions were blossoming beneath his graying prison clothes. Hastings sat a few tables away, staring at him with those baleful, blood-red eyes. Most had learned to revere Nero, but it had been an unspoken truth between them since the first night that the younger boy ranked higher in intimidation.

"Nero Corvis," one of the officers greeted without a hint of friendliness. Nero was almost disappointed it wasn't Charlie today. He enjoyed messing with that guy.

"Barrius," he corrected, not for the first time. The officers didn't flinch, nor did they acknowledge his contradiction; they simply reached to haul him from his chair.

He would have let them if they'd been alone in his dormitory, but here, in front of his peers, he couldn't allow himself to be shoved around. Shoving off the officers' grips, Nero kicked his chair back and then stalked out of the cafeteria as if he were the one in charge. The ache in his arm made him wonder if Hastings had sent him a cruel farewell bruise.

Once removed from the cafeteria, the officers didn't allow Nero to walk on his own. They grabbed either of his arms, guiding him through the white-tiled halls as if they had any real control over him. With the flick of his limbs, Nero could have incapacitated both men. Even at the age of fifteen he was taller than both, his shoulders broad enough that he was often mistaken for a twenty-year-old.

Yet, there was no desire in him to rebel. Though he hated confinement, he'd grown comfortable with it. In three years, he'd built a reputation, and he wasn't sure how easily he could accomplish such a feat if they threw him in an adult prison...or something worse.

When they entered the visitation wing, Nero expected to find his mother waiting. A feeble part of him hoped her unplanned arrival would coincide with his freedom, but the moment they stepped into the desolate room, he knew his mother wasn't present. Her calming ambience would have permeated the air. Instead, the visitor's area was occupied by two bickering men who immediately quieted upon Nero's entrance.

"H-hello," the shorter man choked, fumbling with his clipboard. It nearly slipped from his hands. Nero didn't bother to withhold his snort. "This is Nero Corvis, correct?"

"*Barrius.*"

"Seems like that's the only word he knows how to say," the officer on his left muttered. Nero's fists clenched, preparing for a punch, but then he noticed the way the second mysterious man observed him—and that the second mysterious man had red hair and eyes, even brighter than Hastings's.

"You're one of those Wackos."

The man smiled with enough kindness to give Nero an actual chill. He disguised it by wrenching free from the officers' clutches and looking at the men squarely.

"You're here to recruit me."

The red-eyed man dipped his chin. "We are here to recruit you."

"Good. I'd rather be wreaking havoc than sitting in a cell." Nero's scowl shifted between the officers, both of whom slowly succumbed to discomfort. "Can I start by smashing these two assholes' heads?"

"We aren't terrorists, boy," the shorter man snipped, hugging his clipboard to his chest to prevent it from slipping. Now standing a few feet from him, Nero realized the man *gleamed*, as if he'd just emerged from a pool of *oil*. He almost blurted a crude comment, but then he caught the similarity between the man's hair and eyes. Though they were both plain and dark, they were the same exact hue, like Nero's gray hair and eyes had settled into the same exact hue.

"And we don't condone violence," the man continued, his head held high. "We are administrators from Periculand Training School, and you will treat us with respect. We'll take him now."

"Take me where?" Nero questioned as the officers took simultaneous steps backward. "To the—the *training school?*"

"Yes, actually," the red man said, raising his hand. Nero tensed, anticipating physical force, but the Wacko—because he was still convinced they could be nothing else—merely gestured toward the door, the exit he'd hoped to step through for years. Now that the opportunity was presented to him, he wanted to retreat to his cell instead. It wasn't fear—no, Nero Barrius wasn't afraid of anything. But what if his mother couldn't find him? What if she hadn't been informed of his relocation?

"Fine," he finally grunted, because though they hadn't touched him, he didn't get the impression this was optional. Stomping past the men, he plowed through the *VISITOR'S EXIT.* Charlie waited in the hall beyond, lounging in a swivel chair and playing catch with himself. The ball flung through the air before shooting back toward him. Nero wouldn't have thought it odd if the ball weren't made of metal—and if the ball had actually hit the wall before rebounding.

Obviously, he had witnessed something he shouldn't have, because the officer hastily pocketed the ball and bolted to his feet, face contorted with shock and guilt.

"Uh, Nero… What are you…" His question fizzled at the sight of the two men following the boy through the open doorway.

"I'm leaving." Nero smirked at the way the officer's mouth gaped. "These two terrorists have taken me under their wing. Don't worry—after I've been trained, I'll be back."

Charlie swallowed, but he didn't have the chance to beg on his knees for absolution before the oily man scurried through the metal detector.

"We must be going. We're on a very tight schedule. Mr. Periculy will send you all the paperwork through the web!" he called before disappearing from the hallway.

"Who still calls it *the web*?" Charlie mumbled, clearly perplexed.

"Fraco does, apparently," the red man said with a smile before following his colleague. Nero would have been tempted to mock *the web* or the man whose name was *Fraco* if he hadn't heard that other name—Mr. Periculy. It had been years, but Nero would never forget the eerie, pink-haired man he'd met during his first evening in juvie. If the red man and Fraco *knew* him and *worked* for him, Nero had to admit he was a little—just a little—nervous.

"You said you're *not* terrorists?" Nero questioned as he watched the greasy rat Fraco attempt to open the van door. "Your sketchy white van says otherwise."

"Nah," was the first word that emanated from within the vehicle once the door finally slid aside. Three teenagers sat on the gray seats, and the one with the puke-green hair had spoken. "I'd say this thing screams pedophiles more than terrorists."

"Wouldn't be surprised," Nero muttered, eyes flitting toward the red man, who had assumed the driver's seat. "That guy fits the profile."

The red man didn't even glance back as he started the engine. "I do have ears, Mr. Corvis."

Nero's jaw clenched at that name. He wanted to contradict the man, but then the puke-haired boy opened his mouth again.

"Corvis? Is your mom a wedding planner?"

"No."

"You sure? My mom's new wedding planner looks just like you—'cept her hair's not as gray."

Nero forced his expression to remain stony, even though his insides roiled. Throughout his childhood, he'd always been told he and his mother had an uncanny resemblance. Now the only difference would have been their hair. And now, apparently, his mother was a wedding planner and he knew nothing of it.

"Let's make haste, Mr. Corvis," Fraco commanded as he scrambled into the passenger's seat. Nero was inclined to do the opposite—especially since the man had called him *Corvis*—but if these people were his new terrorist *allies*, he couldn't afford to treat them with the same hostility as his peers in juvie.

Still, making haste proved a tricky feat for Nero. His height and girth made it difficult to squeeze into the van, and once he'd plopped onto the bench facing the rear, it became clear only he and the puke-haired boy would fit there together comfortably. The other two teens were subjected to the back row, positioned as far from each other as possible.

"Don't get too close," the puke-haired kid advised, squishing himself against the wall. His hand grazed the metal, and Nero's eyes widened when it began to *melt*. "Unless you enjoy being burned by acid."

"Acid?"

"Acid Affinity." He flicked his finger, projecting a few drops of clear liquid at the ceiling. The fabric coating it began to disintegrate, fizzling with enough volume that Fraco whipped around in his seat to gawk.

"Mr. Byle—what are you doing? The usage of your Affinity to destroy Periculand property is strictly prohibited!"

The kid shrugged in response. "Sorry—accident." When his murky green eyes landed on Nero, the mischief in them confirmed it was no accident. "Dave. You?"

"Nero. Have you been part of this terrorist organization long?"

"Terrorist organization?" the girl in the back seat repeated, her dark eyebrows raised. Nero assumed her features were the same deep brown that his own had once been, but then a few rays of sunlight touched her hair through the window, giving it an eggplant-like glimmer. "Didn't you do any research when your hair and eyes started to change?"

"Didn't you see I was in *prison*?"

The girl's thin lips curled scornfully. "I would have found a way to do research."

"Hm, sounds like you're a lost cause."

"What is that supposed to mean?"

"I think he knows." Nero jabbed his thumb in Dave's direction as the kid chortled.

"Oh, do I. Jia and I have been in the same school for years. She's the world's biggest nerd. Won a metal for it and everything."

"I won first place at the *history fair*," the girl, Jia, corrected, glaring at him down her upturned nose. "Three times, if you want to get technical."

"Yeah, and I'm sure that accomplishment will go down in history," Dave snorted.

Nero, despite his will to remain nonchalant, found a

chuckle rising in his throat. Thankfully, he managed to transform it into a cough as Fraco snapped, "There will be no bullying, Mr. Byle! Do not fret, Miss Chen. Academic achievements are praised at Periculand Training School."

"*Academics?*" Nero repeated in disgust. "I thought we were going to a terrorist training school—not an *actual* school."

"We aren't terrorists, Mr. Corvis," Fraco singsonged. "And even if you lack academic skills, you will enjoy the school Mr. Periculy has created. There will be ample opportunity for you to practice your Affinity."

"What's your power?" Nero pried, rotating his head toward the man and squinting at the blinding sheen of his skin.

"That is irrele—"

"He's got a *grease* Affinity," Dave said with a snicker. "Which is useless. But if you wanna talk about badass Affinities, *he's* got a rock Affinity."

Nero followed Dave's gesture toward the boy sitting in the back with Jia—although, it was hard to call him a *boy*. Dave definitely looked fifteen, but this other kid was massive enough to be in his late teens—almost as giant as Nero. Where he was solid muscle, this other guy was solid fat, a human boulder that could have posed a real challenge in a fight.

"What exactly can he do with this rock Affinity?" Nero inquired.

Dave opened his mouth, but before he could produce a sound, the window on boulder-boy's right suddenly shattered, spraying glass into the van. Jia and Fraco screamed at the same pitch—Fraco's voice higher, maybe—and Dave spouted more acid onto the ceiling in response, but the red man didn't react in the slightest. The van drove on undeterred while Nero stared intently at the fist-sized rock now perched in boulder-boy's lap.

"That, apparently," the red man said pleasantly.

Tossing the rock casually at Nero, boulder-boy brushed glass off his legs and shot Jia an apologetic glance. Nero didn't wait for her reaction; instead, he studied the dirty rock in his hands, turning it over to inspect it for some abnormality. As far as he could tell, the rock itself was perfectly ordinary, but boulder-boy certainly was not. Somehow, he had *summoned* the rock, as if by magic. The concept seemed as unnatural as—and maybe more deadly than—Hastings's abilities.

"Mr. Craig!" Fraco fumed, his voice still cracking from the scare. "The usage of your Affinity to destroy Periculand property is strictly prohibited! Mr. Periculy will be furious!"

"I believe you're more furious than Mr. Periculy will be, Fraco," the red man stated. "In fact, he's been wanting to buy new vans for months now. Perhaps this will give him an adequate reason to."

"What's your power?" Nero demanded, chucking the rock back at boulder-boy. He assumed the kid must have caught it with his superpowers, but he didn't care to watch since all his attention now fixated on the red man. "Something satanic, I hope."

"I fear I'll disappoint you, Nero"—he shot a polite smile over his shoulder—"but, Jia, you would enjoy my Affinity."

"Time travel," she blurted, perking in her seat and thrusting glass shards from her lap in the process.

"No, it's nothing quite so—"

"What's *your* Affinity?" Dave asked Nero before the man could finish. The only reason he acknowledged the kid was because he no longer cared what the red man could do. If it wasn't violent and that nerdy girl would like it, Nero wasn't interested.

"What's it to you?" he huffed, his posture stiffening with defensiveness.

"Just curious—unless...you don't *know* your Affinity. That would be embarrassing."

"Of course I know it," Nero insisted—because he did, and because he couldn't let them think he didn't. Still, he had no reason to divulge the information yet. Secrets were a power in themselves. Juvie had taught him that much.

"Yes, of course he knows it," Fraco chimed in. "Why do you think he would have ended up in a juvenile detention center if not for his Affinity?"

"You went to juvie for using your Affinity?" Dave questioned, head cocking to the side. "Were you tortured?"

He thought of Hastings but then shook his head. "No. You think anyone stands a chance against me?"

"Little girls certainly don't," the red man said with enough complacency that Nero almost reached over the seats to punch him.

"You used your Affinity on a *little girl?*" Dave repeated in disbelief. "I mean, I've used my Affinity to hurt girls, but never *little* ones. You're an animal."

From anyone else, it might have sounded like revulsion, but this kid's inflection was one of awe.

"Yes, well, I'm not sure what you expected of Mr. Corvis when we told you we'd be retrieving him from a juvenile prison," Fraco sneered. "Of course, he wouldn't have been there for so long if he weren't one of us. He doomed himself by utilizing his Affinity unlawfully."

Though his first instinct was to growl at the man's snooty

tone, the words sparked a question in Nero's mind, one he'd longed to uncover the answer to for years.

"What do you mean I wouldn't have been there so long?"

Fraco swallowed and then fiddle with his clipboard. "Do you really think you would have been subject to an indefinite sentence for domestic violence if you weren't an Affinity? Why do you think you went directly to the detention center before receiving a proper trial? Once they realized what you are, they didn't want to give you an opportunity for escape. They used your misdemeanor as an excuse to keep you locked up until—"

"Until what?" Nero prompted when the explanation abruptly stopped.

"Nothing!"

"Until you turn eighteen," Jia said over Fraco's frantic denial. "That's when they move you from juvie to the real prison—the research facilities."

"Research facilities?"

"That is enough of that!" Fraco proclaimed. As if on cue, the van rolled to a stop, now positioned at the end of a short driveway. Overgrown plants reached toward them from either side like hundreds of ghostly arms. Although the small trailer home buried in the weeds seemed awfully small for an entire terrorist organization, Nero thought it looked shady enough to be a terrorist hideout. He was prepared to exit the van and assert himself as a powerful part of this organization when Fraco snapped, "Stay in the van!"

"Why?" Nero demanded instantly.

"Because," the greasy man grunted as he grappled with the handle of the passenger's side door, "Mr. Certior needs to retrieve Mr. Watkins, and I need to inspect the damage Mr. Craig has inflicted on this van!"

All the formal name calling was starting to give Nero a headache. When the two adults finally exited the vehicle, Fraco muttering loudly and the red man chuckling quietly, Nero threw open the door beside him and hopped onto the weed-infested pavement.

"*Mr. Corvis—*"

"He may come with me, Fraco," the red man said from the other side of the van.

Fraco's mouth flew open, but then his gaze landed on the ruined window, glass shards protruding where the pane had once been, and he moaned, all protests forgotten.

After jumping his eyebrows at the other teens, Nero stalked around the van to join the red man's walk to the front door.

"When I first met Fraco," the man said as Nero stepped in line with him, "I thought I would avoid him at all costs. Now, I've found myself requesting tasks as his companion willingly. Free entertainment, Mr. Corvis."

Nero's brow creased as he tried to gauge the man. "I would be nervous that you let me join you if I wasn't sure I could demolish you in a fight."

The man laughed as they halted before the front door. "No doubt you could. I've heard plenty about your abilities. I do wonder…if you've heard anything about mine. Does the name Aethelred ring any bells?"

"What is that—some weird code name?"

"Of sorts…" Aethelred said before turning his attention to the door. He lifted his fist to knock but then paused, his face scrunching with concern. "I sense something is… strange."

"Is that your power—*sensing things*? No wonder I've never heard of you. But since you know so much about me, why don't I demonstrate my power?"

Before the man could object, Nero lifted his leg and thrust his foot into the flimsy door, blasting it inward. His triumph shattered when it remained on its hinges.

"Mr. Corvis! What are you doing?" Fraco's voice rang from afar. "Mr. Periculy will not be pleased if we owe civilians money for damaged property!"

Nero didn't really care about that. In fact, he didn't give a damn about anything anyone said in that moment, because his demonstration with the door hadn't just displayed his abilities; it had also opened a viewing portal to this dilapidated trailer home and the heinous acts unfolding within.

"Gimme his address," the larger man roared as he pinned a teenage boy against the peeling wallpaper. "I need to silence him before he starts spreadin' rumors that disgrace me."

"I don't—know his address," the boy stammered, blood dripping from his nostrils and mouth. His pale face looked even worse than Albie's did after Nero's periodic beatings. "But I know he won't talk. No one will know."

"I always knew you were a pathetic excuse for a son," the older man sneered as he delivered a punch to the boy's gut. With barely a layer of fat to conceal his organs, the skinny boy doubled over and crumbled to the floor.

Whenever a kid at juvie collapsed in this way, Nero would smile with vindictive mirth, but he found no pleasure in this boy's pain. Maybe it was because he took the beating well—without crying, without pleading—or maybe it was because Nero knew what it was like to suffer the wrath of an abusive father. It was a different type of abuse, but scarring either way.

"Get me the address or you'll suffer worse than this," the

man warned, kicking his son with his muddy boot, "and so will your little—"

Nero almost faltered, curious as to what *little* thing this father would abuse along with the boy, but he was already mid-swing, and his fist collided with the back of the man's head before he could complete his sentence. Like an ugly weed, he wilted to the ground, unruly hair splayed over his face and mouth open to display crooked teeth.

The boy didn't look up at first. His eyes remained on his father, but there was no shock in them, only abhorrence— and streaks of pink.

"I hope you don't plan to leave me here with him like this. He won't be thrilled when he wakes up," the boy said as his head slowly craned upward. The structure of his face was thin, but his cheeks were round, like a squirrel storing nuts. There was nothing nature-related that Nero could compare his hair to, though. The blond strands looked like they'd been infused with pink taffy.

In juvie, Nero probably would have been the one to pummel a kid like this. In juvie, however, he hadn't been exposed to the horrors of his peers' home lives.

"Don't tell the others," he grumbled as he extended his hand toward the boy.

Without any shame or embarrassment, the kid placed his dainty fingers in Nero's meaty palm and allowed himself to be hoisted upright. "That you're not a complete asshole, you mean?"

Nero balked at the chilling quality of the kid's tone—and the impossible accuracy of his statement. It was as if this boy had been in the van with them for the past twenty minutes, aware of who the others were and how standoffish Nero had acted with them.

"We should leave now." The boy wiped the blood from his nose. He didn't grant his unconscious father another glance before waltzing toward the door and nodding at Aethelred. "Certior."

"Mr. Watkins," the man returned, but when Nero gave him a questioning glare, he shrugged. "I've never met him. Don't ask *me* how he knows my name."

Nero grumbled incoherently about the strangeness of this day until they reached the driveway, where the boy spun around to face him with a serious expression.

"I won't tell if you won't tell." He didn't have to raise his pink eyebrows for Nero to understand what he meant, and Nero didn't have to give a verbal confirmation for the kid to know it was a deal. "I'm Jerry. Nice to meet you, Nero."

As promised, Jerry didn't breathe a word about Nero's act of kindness. In a way, he almost wished the boy had, though. Yes, it had been a rare, righteous rage, but it had also been violence. He wanted these other kids to know he wouldn't hesitate with aggression.

Clearly, Jerry didn't want anyone knowing anything about *him.* When he entered the van, he didn't say a word, and he sat as far from boulder-boy as he could, practically squeezing himself against a displeased Jia. Still, no matter how squished she was, her annoyance would never surpass Fraco's. He spent the next fifteen minutes of driving ranting about how precious the van was and how much of a hazard the glass was and how he hoped boulder-boy—who Nero learned was named Haldor—would accidentally cut himself as punishment.

Fed up, Nero was ready to drown out Fraco's squawking

voice and take a nap when the van parked again. Unlike the last stop, they'd now arrived at a well-maintained home that looked too much like the Millers' for Nero to admire it. In fact, the neighborhood might have even been his father's. If it was, he didn't want to know; he remained in the van until Aethelred and Fraco returned, this time with two teens at their heels.

"If I hear he's been injured in any way, I will find you, and you will regret this," a young feminine voice threatened when the van door glided open. "Even if he injures himself, you'll pay for it."

"Relax, Lav. I think I'm old enough to fend for myself," the boy droned, rolling his eyes. The irises were almost as pukey as Dave's, an unappealing mix of gray and khaki, twin to the color of his moppy hair. Even tanner than Nero, his skin was the same tone as the girl glued to his hip, who Nero assumed was his sister. She was not nearly as unappealing; though she seemed a few years younger, her hair was cool like coffee, and there was a fierceness to her that Nero could appreciate.

"There's no need to fear, girl," Fraco assured in a condescending voice. "No one gets hurt in Periculand unless they're asking for it. Many do, but that's beside the point."

"If Ruse doesn't look exactly like he does right now when I get there—"

"Yikes, sis, you know that'll be impossible. I've barely hit puberty," the unappealing boy, Ruse, joked as he nudged her arm.

"You can make your assessment in two years, Miss Dispus," Fraco said, shooing her away with his clipboard and the subsequent oil that spewed with the motion. "Until then, Mr. Dispus will accompany us and you will scurry back into your house to laze about with your grandparents."

"That sounds oddly sexual—and incesty," Ruse said with a wrinkled nose. "Have fun."

"Let me come," the girl insisted, grabbing Fraco's sleeve only for her hand to slide off due to the greasiness. "You know I have an Affinity. Why wait to take me? The government might get me first, and I know what they do to Affinities."

"Your grandparents will keep you safe, Miss Dispus," Fraco said as he wrestled with the door handle yet again.

"My grandparents are nearly ninety, and my presence will put them in *danger*."

Finally hauling the door open, Fraco gave her a curt smile. "Well, there's no reason to fret, then. If they're ninety, they'll die soon with or without your dangerous presence."

Ruse pivoted his head toward his sister and arched his gross eyebrows. "I give you permission to break your vow not to hurt innocent people."

"I wouldn't call him innocent," Lavisa growled, at which Fraco scrambled into his seat and slammed the door.

"Mr. Dispus, quickly!"

Nero watched in disgust as Ruse reached to hug his sister…and then burst out in snickers when Lavisa shoved him away to storm back toward her house.

"You just got rejected by your sister," Nero derided. Dave joined in readily, but Jerry didn't look remotely amused. His face was as blank now as it had been throughout the drive, but there was a hint of curious confusion in his gaze as he scrutinized the newest addition to the terrorist van.

"Or you could say I got friend-zoned, if we're continuing the incest joke," Ruse said whimsically.

Nero's lips formed a sneer as his laughter subsided.

"We're not. I was mocking you, idiot."

Instead of cowering, the boy shrugged and then hopped into the van. "Cool, I guess, if that's what you're into."

Dave looked flabbergasted, but Nero couldn't show his bewilderment. This kid was trying to mess with him, and Nero would not be messed with. Not anymore.

Conspicuously, he kicked out his leg to trip Ruse. Like the dumbass he was, the kid stumbled over it, flopping gracelessly into the space between Haldor and Jerry.

"Oh, shit-sticks," Ruse blurted as he pushed away from the seat, scrambling across the floor of the van. "There's a...a..."

"A person," Jerry finished flatly. "Are you surprised?"

Ruse blinked—and blinked again. He blinked at least fifty times at Jerry before pitifully spluttering, "A little."

"This is Blaire, everyone," the pink-haired boy droned, motioning toward the vacant spot on the bench beside him. Nero sat forward and squinted, thinking maybe her appearance blended with the shadows of the van, but there was no one there. "She's invisible, as you can see. She didn't want anyone to know she's here, but I don't really care."

"I like that," Nero said, referring to Jerry's lack of care. When the boy fixed him with a stare, Nero realized how stupid the comment sounded, so he added, "Invisibility could be useful...for terrorist purposes."

"Terrorist purposes?" Ruse repeated as he sagged against the side of the van. When he noticed the spot Dave had burned and the glass pooled on the floor around him, he began spasming with alarm.

"We are not terrorists!" Fraco almost shrieked. Clearing his throat, he tapped his clipboard on the steering wheel. "Onward, Mr. Certior. We need to return to Periculand and purge these misconceptions from the students' minds. You will soon see, Mr. Corvis, that Periculand is not a place of terror. It is, in fact, the best place on Earth."

4

Manipulation of Mortification

"I think I'm gonna hate myself for saying this, but Periculand is, in fact, the best place on Earth," said that annoying prick, *Ruse*, as the students entered the cafeteria the next morning.

Nero wasn't sure how he'd ended up so close to the babbling freak, but he knew no matter how far he got, Ruse's voice would find his ears. Somehow, it was even more obnoxious than Fraco's, and Nero had to exercise an extreme amount of control to prevent his fist from demolishing the nearest gray wall. They were so similar to the walls at juvie that he felt as if he hadn't left that place—or as if he'd left that place to enter an even worse prison that Ruse Dispus and Fraco Leve inhabited.

"Just *look* at that buffet," the boy gushed as he weaved through the brightly-colored tables. Dave followed him, nodding in ardent agreement, and Nero scoffed aloud at the sight. Between the van ride the previous day and the fact that Dave was his roommate, Nero had almost started to *like* the kid. Watching him frolic around with Ruse now reminded Nero that no one was to be liked and no one was to be trusted. Without glancing at the buffet, he stomped through the cafeteria in search of an empty table.

"What happened to your arms?" a silky voice cooed, snapping him out of his furious daze. Whipping toward the voice, he found a girl sitting alone at a yellow table. It was hard to call her a *girl*, though. Her appearance was that of a goddess: long legs crossed delicately, fully-developed chest popping beneath her "Periculand Training School" t-shirt, and hair that sparkled like a sea of gold flowing down her back.

Nero hadn't seen any attractive girls since he was twelve.

With a predatory grin, he assumed the seat beside her.

"Got into a fight." He flexed his muscles and the mosaic of bruises decorating them. "I won, obviously."

"Obviously," she echoed, batting her gold-coated eyelashes. They matched the hue of her irises perfectly, and the longer he stared into them, the less he felt like flexing. His only desire, as he gazed into the seductive depths of her eyes, was to melt *into* her.

"At it already, Orla?"

Shaking his head, Nero focused on another girl strolling behind the goddess, a green tray of food in her hands. The yearning that had formed in the pit of his stomach vanished completely, replaced by revulsion.

"Are you *blind*?" he sneered at the girl with the milk-white eyes. The question had been rhetorical, of course; there were no pupils in those eyes, so she must have been blind. It almost seemed like she was looking right at him, though, and the way she dodged tables, chairs, and people should have been impossible.

"Not blind enough to miss that Orla's using her Affinity on you," the girl said blandly. "Tell him, Belven, how you wooed your way into every primary boy's pants last year."

"Not *every* boy." The goddess, Orla, arched her gilded

eyebrows at the guy now approaching their table. Nero knew he compared a lot of people's hair to puke, but this kid's had to have been the worst. His head looked like he'd dipped it in nuclear gasoline—neon yellow infused with oil brown, a few stray strands of black peeking through the mess.

"I see why you didn't want to bang this one," Nero huffed. "It's fortunate you found a blind girl. No one else would be so desperate."

Orla emitted a laugh, smooth as molten gold. "Oh, you're funny. Though it's not always looks I value—*talents* attract me, as well." Her gaze lingered on his arms for a few seconds before she regarded the new guy. He stood beside the blind girl, looking stupidly bemused. "Avner's are…astonishing. But he's with Zeela now, and I would never intrude."

The blind freak, who Nero assumed was Zeela, pursed her lips in dissatisfaction. "C'mon, Av. Let's move before Jamad comes over here and gets sucked into her web."

"Webs can't suck—but mouths can," Orla purred, wiggling her eyebrows at Avner. The kid stumbled after his girlfriend, dazed and clumsy—pathetic. Nero, of course, wouldn't admit that he, too, had been a bit stunned by the magnetism of her voice…and the reaction her innuendo elicited.

"Now, you," Orla prompted, leaning forward. If the uniforms weren't so damn concealing, she would have been at the perfect angle for Nero's eyes to feast. "What's *your* talent?"

He inclined toward her, pulling up the sleeve of his t-shirt to brandish his bicep, when something banged the back of his head.

Macaroni flew onto the table, though not before dousing him in warm cheese. It oozed down his cheeks, soaking his hair into a limp blob. Orla, instead of squealing at the food that had sprayed her t-shirt, actually grinned.

"Hello," she greeted, her gaze fixed beyond Nero. When he craned his neck, allowing cheese to slip onto his eyelids, he saw Dave had materialized behind him. The kid's swampy eyes bulged in awe, and his hands still held the tray that had bumped into Nero's head and showered him with macaroni.

"H-hi," he stuttered, unaware that he'd humiliated Nero to an unforgivable extent. The embarrassment alone would have been enough to tempt the brute with violence, but then, in his stupor, Dave's fingers began dripping acid. Right onto Nero's scalp.

Luckily, his hair—and the cheese that coated it—served as a barrier, but Nero still felt the acid gnawing away at the strands, threatening to singe his skin. Jumping from his seat and scrambling away from Dave, he threw his head around wildly, trying to purge the acid from his hair like a dog shaking off water. Orla's delicately devious laughter filled the air again, this time chorused with Dave's chuckles. It enraged Nero enough that he reached for Dave, planning to hurl him across the room—until a thin hand grasped his forearm, distracting him from his fury.

"You need to go to the nurse," Jerry said, his pinkish eyes dark with severity. "I don't know what type of acid he secretes, but some can be fatal."

The retort "Nothing can kill me" waited to expel from Nero's mouth, but Jerry was probably right. As much as Nero hated to acknowledge that anyone else could be right, he saw this act of kindness for what it was: the repaying of a debt.

Even so, he was inclined to disregard the advice and exact his revenge on Dave until he noticed the kid was already punishing himself.

Food tray abandoned, he'd plopped into Nero's chair fallen limp against the table, his head in a pool of melted cheese. Drool seeped from his gaping mouth as he stared at Orla like a zombie. She didn't seem perturbed; a smile was plastered on her perfect lips, her manicured fingers twirling through her endless curls.

Nero had assumed Dave sabotaged his chat with the girl to claim her as his own, but apparently he'd surrendered to her trance—the same trance Nero had fallen for.

That, he realized, was the real embarrassment—that he could succumb to mindlessness with such ease. Throughout his life, Nero hadn't had control over much, but he had always commanded his own mind. This girl had the power to seize that from him in a way he actually craved.

Disgusted with Orla, Dave, this place, and himself, Nero staggered through the cafeteria, vowing never to fall prey to her seduction again. He had been the alpha in juvie, and it would be no different here. He would rule this school, one way or another. And since Orla had found pleasure in wrapping him around her finger, he would return the favor and wrap her around his. Tightly.

"You're not dead. What a shame," the girl from the van, Jia, greeted when Nero stepped into the training gymnasium that afternoon. In the fluorescent lights, her hair was more prominently purple, a shade not too distant from the cargo pants the Mentals wore. Jia was a Physical like Nero, though, as denoted by their matching rust-orange pants.

"I'm kidding," she amended after Nero growled. She and the other primaries from the van were huddled at the back of the crowd forming on the mats. Among them, Haldor juggled a rock, Jerry observed the scene emotionlessly, Dave swayed in disorientation, and the other girl, Blaire—who Nero had yet to actually *see*—was probably invisible if she was there at all.

"Jerry said you were injured," Jia continued, nodding toward the pink-haired boy, who didn't react to the sound of his name. "Glad you're okay."

"I was always okay," Nero grumbled, crossing his arms. The statement was a lie. By the time he'd stumbled into the nurse's office, his head throbbed as if he'd been branded, and he felt a dizzy sort of nausea that the nurse attributed to hunger. After healing the burn with his Affinity, the nurse had insisted Nero eat some crackers. Even though he'd felt like a five-year-old doing so, he'd savored it. Long enough to skip all his morning classes.

Now that he was back with his peers, he wished he'd taken advantage of his injury for the rest of the day. Between Jia's sympathetic gaze, Dave's presence, and Fraco's squawky voice beckoning for everyone's attention, Nero's head ached worse than it had from the burn.

"Your hair doesn't look okay," Ruse said as he stepped beside Nero and stood on his toes to examine his head. "You look like one of those monks, bald on top—"

"Shut *up*," Nero barked at the same time as Fraco. With the volume of both voices, the gymnasium finally lulled into silence, eyes darting between the two, wondering which they were listening to.

After gifting Nero with an awkward nod of gratitude, Fraco straightened his suit jacket and lifted his pointy nose. "Now, primaries," were the only words Nero acknowledged. He wasn't in the mood to listen to one of the man's condescending speeches. He *was* in the mood to plan Dave's demise—and Orla's. If he could cause both simultaneously, he would be doubly satisfied.

As Fraco explained the self-explanatory purpose of training sessions, Nero searched the mass of abnormally-colored heads for Orla. About a hundred students were present, and she was the only one whose locks held a metallic gleam. His temper flared when he noticed her across the room whispering to yet another boy. This one, with skin like umber and hair like frost, didn't seem as entranced as Dave had. Rather, his lips were curved into a charming grin, willingly engaging in Orla's flirtation.

Idiot, Nero mused to himself. He was tempted not to intervene, as he had initially planned to. If this guy was moronic enough to entertain Orla, Nero would revel in his degradation. Watching it unfold within this training session would be enough to satiate his vengeful desires for the day.

At the same time, a small part of him boiled at the sight of Orla flirting with this other boy. It was probably a lingering effect of her enchantment, but she didn't seem to use any of that magic on this other guy. She almost seemed like she *enjoyed* her conversation with him, and for some reason, that made Nero *jealous*.

"But first, is there anyone who would like to demonstrate their Affinity in front of everyone?" Fraco asked, scanning the crowd almost nervously. It was a miracle no one's hand immediately shot up; as soon as the question was posed, schemes began forming in Nero's mind of how he would volunteer and amaze everyone with his superhuman strength. Orla wouldn't look at the frosty-haired boy then. Her eyes would be only for Nero, and he would take charge of the school—

"I'll do it," the guy with the hideous, neon-streaked hair offered, raising his hand slightly as he strolled to the center of the mats. Nero's fists clenched at the boy's easy smile, his casual confidence, the fact that he was so unappealing and yet no one in this room mocked him. A kid like him would have been torn apart in juvie—probably by Nero—but here the students muttered animatedly about him and his impressive Affinity. *Avner*, they called him, and he was *so powerful*, they said.

Nothing could be more powerful than Nero, who had instilled trepidation in a compound of criminals.

Child criminals, he grudgingly reminded himself, two of whom had managed to scare him right back. The boy who could rupture his veins, and the boy who knew his darkest secrets—they were the only other Affinities Nero had ever encountered, and in this moment, they were the only reason he didn't plow through the throng to pummel Avner. Because if this kid's Affinity was *that* impressive…

"What do you want me to do?" Avner asked, looking to Fraco for instruction.

The oily man's mouth flopped open, but before he could utter a sound, Nero brashly exclaimed, "Dye your hair, loser!"

A tense quiet permeated the air. He expected *someone* to laugh—at least Dave. But that imbecile was still in his own world, probably daydreaming about Orla. Jia gave Nero a pitying smile when he peered in her direction, which sparked fury rather than consolation. Jerry remained stone-faced.

"Look who's talking, monk!" a voice called, drawing Nero's gaze toward Orla. It was the frosty-haired kid who had jeered at him, his hand still cupped around his smirking lips.

Avner mimicked the jaunty expression as he motioned to

his hair. "Should I?"

Chuckles fluttered through the gymnasium. Avner's tone had been one of mockery—not mocking his hair but...*Nero.* These petty students were laughing at *Nero.*

"No, Mr. Stromer, you should not dye your hair!" Fraco snapped as the laughter subsided. "Get on with the demonstration."

Still amused by his own joke, Avner stepped into an aggressive stance. Instead of launching forward, he simply raised his hands, discharging a blinding bolt of lightning.

It surged toward the ceiling, colliding with one of the massive lights. Screams punctured the quiet as glass and sparks rained down. A few shards sprinkled Nero's shoulders, but he didn't care. Half the lights in the gymnasium had popped due to the power surge, but there was still more than enough visibility for him to glare at Avner.

He and his friends giggled over his mistake and Fraco's panic. The rest of the students were either startled or dazzled, some hyperventilating while others cheered. Avner's power should have induced a sense of apprehension in Nero, but instead it provoked a need to demolish him. If this Stromer kid could destroy school property without reprimand, Nero could sure as hell smash his face to pieces.

Slamming through a group of frazzled students, Nero stomped toward the middle of the room. Before he could emerge from the crowd and challenge Stromer, however, his vision caught onto a sight that paralyzed him. The frosty-haired boy had deserted Orla to converse with Avner, but she wasn't alone. Someone else had joined her side—someone who looked exactly like Nero. Someone who...*was* Nero.

A debilitating sense of vertigo washed over his brain as he stared at *himself* speaking to Orla with wryly curled lips. The expression was too pleasant for his face, and his posture was awkward and exaggerated, as if he wasn't used to the size of his body. Whatever his doppelgänger muttered provoked a giddy grin onto her face, and Nero—the real Nero— wondered if he was being shown some cruel reality of what he would look like if he weren't always so hostile.

Then the image of him flickered.

It wasn't a hallucination—no. His double wasn't disappearing; he was morphing. Ever so slightly, the second Nero's nose would narrow or his hair would lighten or his muscles would deflate. Someone else had taken the shape of his body.

Nero could not allow that.

Revitalized, he stormed through the last layer of students and lurched at the imposter. With a yelp, the other Nero plummeted to the ground, his body shrinking beneath the real Nero's weight. When he pulled his first back to wham the impersonator's face, he saw it had completely transformed. The strong jaw had weakened, the thick eyebrows had thinned, and the dark gray irises had become diluted, now a sickly, greenish tan.

"*Dispus,*" Nero ground out, his fist suspended in the air. The boy trembled, his face a picture of terror. It was so gratifying, how rapidly the fear materialized. This punch would be a warning, not just to Ruse but to all of Periculand, that Nero would not tolerate disrespect.

"I wonder," he said, his voice carrying through the hushed gymnasium, "if you'll be able to transform a broken nose."

"I...don't really wonder that," Ruse countered, squirming. "Let's not bother to find out."

Manic glee spread over Nero's face. "No, let's."

Flexing his muscles, he prepared to smother Dispus with the fullness of his strength. Since beating up his half-siblings, Nero had perfected the art of an attack. He knew which hits invoked the best reactions, the most pain. Those would be his targets now. He would *demonstrate* for this crowd what true power was. Not some little lightning trick, but the authority of aggression, of ruthlessness, of agony.

His fist arced downward.

And then his body convulsed.

By the time he had fully comprehended what had happened, he was lying supine, staring at the broken lights and the multitude of faces peeking down at him. Muscles twitched. His joints ached. He felt as if he'd touched an electrical socket, and essentially he had, because Avner Stromer had *electrocuted* him.

Some seemed concerned, but many of the students looming over him *snickered.* Dave, Nero realized with spite, was one of them.

"Whoa." Beside Nero, Ruse sat up and ran his hands over his arms. His shirt had stretched and ripped a bit from his earlier transformation. Nero wanted to stretch *him* until he ripped.

"Sorry." Avner winced as he approached them. "I didn't mean to get both of you."

"Nah, that was sick," Ruse said, studying his skin. "*Electrifying,* one could say."

Avner let out an affable laugh. "You could say that, yeah. And, uh, I am sorry to you, too."

Nero's brain felt so fried that it took him a few moments to recognize that the kid was addressing him—and *apologizing.* As if he could ever forgive such a public offense.

"I don't usually like to use my Affinity on people—"

"I do," Nero snarled before grabbing Avner by the ankle—or trying to grab Avner by the ankle. His depth perception was slightly off, so he only grasped air. Befuddled by the miscalculation, Nero stared at his hand but didn't try again. He had disgraced himself enough for one day, and everyone knew it. Those who had been worried before chortled along with the rest now. The entire gymnasium delighted in his failure.

Except Jerry. Other than Fraco—who was freaking out, as usual—Jerry was the only person who hadn't found merriment in Nero's defeat. He stood on the edge of the crowd, watching with slightly parted lips, like words were on the tip of his tongue but he couldn't quite get them out.

Nero didn't need to hear them to understand. He'd stumbled upon Jerry's altercation with his father, and he'd empathized with that. Maybe this public mortification was something Jerry could empathize with in return.

Never had Nero imagined his only ally would be a skinny, squirrelly kid with bubblegum pink hair.

Vilified and jittery, Nero departed training early and went to the one place where he knew no one would look for him: the library.

With the entirety of the school still in the gymnasium, the library was completely desolate except for the librarian. So engrossed in the book she was reading, her teal blue head didn't even flinch when Nero entered.

It wouldn't have mattered if she had noticed him or even if she'd commanded him to return to training. Nothing could force him back there, not today. He hadn't *fled*—he wasn't *hiding.* No, he just couldn't stand to breathe the same air as those assholes anymore. If he'd spent one more moment in that room with Ruse, he would have strangled the kid—and Avner, too. In fact, he was tempted to stomp back there and end them both.

But…his plan was in motion now, and he could only eliminate one target at a time. After touching every bookshelf he passed, Nero sat at the table in the farthest corner. Then he waited.

"A peculiar hiding spot," a sleek voice crooned, drawing his head upward. His face had been buried in his hands, and he did his best to look distraught when he met her golden gaze. A half-smirk rested on her lips, and she slipped into the chair across from his with otherworldly elegance. "Sulking, Corvis? I expected better from you, but you're just a sad, sad primie."

His jaw tightened at the jab, but he managed to make his voice sullen as he said, "Yeah. I am."

Orla's brows furrowed in confusion as she examined him. "Avner really got into your head, huh? Well, you'll be reassured to know that he gets into my head, as well. If only he would get under my skin—or in it, if you know what I mean."

These taunts were meant to rattle him, but Nero was determined to remain glum. Leaning back in his chair, he gazed up at the second floor of the library wistfully. "He outmatched me. My Affinity will never be as powerful as his."

Orla fidgeted, clearly displeased by his mood. She wanted some flirtatious banter, and honestly, Nero did, too, but he couldn't cave to his desires. If he did, he and Orla would be tumbling amongst the bookshelves, and not in a vengeful manner.

"I know his weakness," she finally whispered, shocking Nero with her conspiratorial tone. "It's his girlfriend, Mensen—it's revolting. He chose that blind rat over *me*. But...what I mean to say is that if you hurt her, you can hurt him."

Nero's eyes drifted to hers, searching for any hint of deceit. Her Affinity wasn't at play here, though; she wasn't trying to seduce him. Maybe because she knew this information would be attractive enough on its own.

"You would like that," he huffed. "If Mensen was out of the way."

"Perhaps," she conceded, lips inching upward. "Or perhaps I'd just like to watch you do it—destroy them, I mean. It might...turn me on."

Heat spread through his gut, but he couldn't surrender to it—not yet. Because his plan was to trick Orla into falling in love with him, and he knew a girl who could have any guy she wanted would only want the one she couldn't have.

"Then I'll have to decline," he said aloofly, his previous despondency hardening into something that made Orla's head cock to the side. "I only do things for my own benefit."

"*Really?*" She licked her lips, turning them to an irresistible shade of pink. Against his will, Nero found himself goggling at them. A glow consumed her cheeks, and her hair seemed to glitter—

"Really," he repeated flatly, straining to keep him body firmly planted in his chair. Most of him wanted to launch over the table and claim her, but it was easier to resist now that he knew what she was doing. "You're dismissed."

"D-*dismissed?*" The revulsion on her face was almost more exciting to him than her sexual suggestions.

"Oh, yes, you didn't catch on?" he mused, eyeing the

bookshelves. "My scent must have been abnormally strong."

Her gaping mouth snapped shut. Her nose twitched in realization. Her face formed a frown, and it was as ugly as anyone else's. "Avner told you—or Jamad—or Mensen—"

"I guessed," he breathed, but it was loud enough for her to hear. Now he really held her interest. "You're a predator. I know because I'm one too, and predators can smell prey. I assumed it must have been part of your Affinity—sniffing out the weak ones."

"So you made yourself seem weak," she sighed, slumping back in her seat. "You knew if you stormed out like a child I'd follow you—easy prey. I guess that means you're not."

"No, I'm not," he agreed, inclining forward to fold his hands on the table. Her scent of milk and honey hung thick in the air, so Nero refrained from breathing through his nose. "I led you here, and you know what that makes you."

Swallowing, Orla stiffened her posture and met his gaze levelly. "What is it you want, Corvis?"

He shrugged. "I just wanna be the hardest victim you ever encounter. In more than one way."

"I see." Her lips pursed, indicating she was up for the challenge. The fearlessness she exuded was uncomfortably alluring. Perhaps this would be a challenge for Nero, as well. He would accept it, like he would accept any challenge, but that wouldn't stop him from relishing this revenge.

"I'll see you around," he said without standing. It took her a moment to process, but once she recognized the second dismissal, her eyes flared in rage. She looked like a feral cat, ready to pounce, and Nero wished she would. He could crush her—or threaten to. Instead, she shoved her chair back and glared at him before strutting away, swaying her hips to tantalize him.

5

The Ruse and The Brute

"Next slide…and next slide… Am I going too fast?" the scrawny teacher asked, his pink eyes glowing in the light of the screen. The hyperactive man reminded Nero too much of Hartman—not that he would have enjoyed this guy's class much regardless. He flipped through the slideshow with such speed that Nero wouldn't have been able to pay attention even if he'd wanted to.

"*Yes*," Jia piped up from the row in front of Nero's. She was the only one in this class of primary Physicals who had taken any notes during the first week of classes, and no one else seemed inclined to join her any time soon. "Can you pause each slide long enough for me to copy it?"

The teacher practically spasmed. "I-I suppose I can do that…"

"Thank you," Jia breathed, hunching over to write furiously in her notebook. Nero rolled his eyes to the left where Dave sat, purposely burning his pencils with acid. Over the past few days, Nero's opinion of his roommate hadn't altered; he still wished to crush him like an insect. The problem was that Dave was a poisonous insect, and Nero couldn't destroy him by physical force alone—at least, not yet.

"Here," a voice whispered, and Nero didn't have to turn

to know Ruse had slipped into the seat on his right. Through-out the week, the kid had assumed so many different forms that Nero had learned to recognize him by his annoying voice rather than his physical appearance. Although he wouldn't have minded smashing the kid's head into a door, he also knew Ruse could become *useful* if Nero determined a way to harness him.

For a moment, he believed Ruse's "here" had been an announcement of his presence, but then he noticed the kid had dropped a folded piece of paper on the table before him. Suspicious, Nero narrowed his eyes at Ruse before carefully prying it open. With the size of his fingers, it was a difficult feat, but once the note lay open before him, he was proud he'd restrained himself enough not to rip it.

Nero, I know you've been avoiding me, but we need to talk. Meet me in the hallway. Now.

No signature was needed for Nero to know who had written the note. She'd sent him similar ones all week, each composed in her stylish scrawl and sprinkled with golden sparkles. The paper even smelled like her—sweet, creamy. Inhaling it was enough to tempt him, but...she needed to be truly desperate. She would be most vulnerable then.

"Not interested," Nero said at a normal volume. A few kids glanced in his direction, but he ignored them as he chucked the crumpled note at Ruse's face. "Tell her."

"I'm not your messenger," he replied, slouching carelessly in his chair. His hair was a vibrant shade of red today, and Nero was prepared to paint the rest of his face to match. "She just cornered me when I was coming back from the bathroom, and it would have been rude to say no. I am a gentleman, after all."

Nero's hands curled into fists, but before he could dole a punch, a second note landed on the table before him as boulder-boy lumbered by. As usual, Haldor said nothing, but Nero was sharp enough to guess Orla had cornered him, as well.

Now, Nero.

A woman of persistence. Nero might have actually been attracted to her resolve—her ambition—but she had played him for a fool, and she would do it again if he let her.

After crinkling the paper, he whipped it at the shape-shifter's face, this time hitting with greater impact.

"Ow," Ruse blurted out like the baby he was. Bringing his hand to his cheek, he gave Nero an affronted look. "I can change my skin, but I can't heal paper cuts, you know. Damn, that stings…"

"Good," Nero snorted, wishing he could see some actual blood. He was considering punching Ruse for fun when a voice caught his attention.

I'm in the hallway with Orla. She wants me to tell you that she wants you…in multiple ways. Sorry— multiple positions. It was meant to be sexy, but I'm butchering it. Somewhat purposely.

Half-petrified, Nero rotated back and forth, searching for the source of the voice. He recognized it as Jerry's, but… Jerry wasn't in this class; he was a Mental, not a Physical. And, somehow, *he'd spoken into Nero's mind.*

Bracing his hands on the table, Nero worked through this baffling truth: Jerry was some kind of…mind messenger.

Most call it mind reading, though that's only half of it, the boy thought to him. *I can project thoughts as well as process them. And I think Belven's going to barge in there and drag you out here by the groin if you don't comply to her wishes within the next few seconds.*

With all the concentration he could muster, Nero thought, *I wouldn't mind so much if she dragged me by the groin.*

I know with uncomfortable clarity what you would and wouldn't mind. Oh, and now she'd like me to tell you that your hair looks good—sorry, sexy from this angle.

Nero whirled around, expecting to find Jerry and Orla framed in the open doorway. Neither was there, though he didn't have to wonder how she would know what his head looked like from behind. Not all of his hair had grown back from Dave's acid accident, which had, of course, been induced by Orla's seduction.

Snarling, Nero flung his chair back. It clattered against the table behind him, silencing the entire room. All whispers subsided, all slide-switching ceased—even Jia had halted her feverous note-taking.

"May I go hook up with a girl in the hallway?" Nero demanded, receiving a few quiet chuckles, most prominently from Dave.

"M-may you what?" the teacher questioned incredulously.

"I'll take that as a yes," he growled, kicking Ruse's chair as he stalked past. The teacher was still spluttering when Nero exited the room, but he didn't care; his sight was set on the end of the hall, where Orla lounged against the wall, twirling her finger through Jerry's pinkish hair.

Unsurprisingly, the mind reader remained unaffected by Orla's display of possessive affection. He stared apathetically ahead, mouth parted enough to reveal his large teeth, almost in a state of boredom when Nero approached.

"She thinks she's got me under her trance," Jerry said, paralyzing Orla's hand mid-twirl. "Really, I was sick of class and thought this would be more entertaining. Not a bad scalp massage, though."

Orla dropped her hand instantly, scowling as redness crept into her cheeks. "That's…manipulative."

"And you're not?" Nero crooned, jumping his eyebrows at her. She fidgeted against the wall but maintained her haughty expression. "This better be good, Belven. I was really enjoying snickering to myself at all those stupid kids in there before you summoned me."

"Sorry to interrupt such pleasure," she said as she examined her gilded fingernails, "but I think you'll enjoy this more."

Impatiently, she fixed Jerry with a glare that likely held more weight than Nero could decipher. She must have thought something vulgar because the mind reader's eyebrows shot up as he said, "Good thing insults don't bother me. I'll leave you two to it."

For some strange reason, Nero felt the urge to thank him. He wasn't sure *why*. He never thanked *anyone*, not even his own mother. But the words had been on his tongue until he'd swallowed them, ashamed of such weak dependency. Jerry understood, and there was a hint of contentment in the curve of his lips as he departed.

With only their breaths to fill the quiet corridor, Nero turned his full attention to Orla. Her golden locks glinted in the light from the triangular windows, and her skin looked tanner against the white walls. Even without her Affinity, she was the most attractive girl he'd ever encountered—or maybe that was part of her Affinity: being attractive, even without the trance.

"You've missed me, huh?"

His assumption startled her, but she recovered quickly,

schooling her features into neutrality. "I just thought you'd want to discuss our common interests."

Nero took a few leisurely steps forward, closing the distance between them. "And what interests are those?"

Her eyelids lowered before she met his gaze again, now with more intensity than before. "Power. Influence. Authority."

"Yes," Nero acknowledged, his body inching toward hers. As a result, she'd flattened her back against the wall, but it seemed more of an invitation than an escape.

He didn't have much experience with girls. There had been one mildly attractive girl who'd shown up in juvie, and of course, Nero had kissed her. She'd been nothing compared to Orla, though, and that had been sloppy, anyway. With Orla, Nero had to be precise.

Tantalizingly, he stroked a finger along her jaw, and then he mentally chided himself for how it made *him* shudder.

"I am...interested in those things," he said as coolly as he could. She didn't seem to have noticed his embarrassing reaction. His touch had frozen her. That was when Nero realized Orla was *always in control*. All of her physical encounters were orchestrated under that magical trance, and so this realness was foreign to her.

Too bad it wasn't real at all.

Dousing the heat building in his core, Nero clutched her head and pushed it to the wall, rough enough to surprise her but gentle enough not to induce pain. "Power, influence, authority—I'd say I have all that right now. Was this what you had in mind?"

From the corner of his eye, he saw her biting her lip when he brought his mouth to her ear. "I was—thinking...for both of us," she managed. He knew what she meant, but he still reveled in how much this frazzled her.

"And how, exactly, can we both rule?"

"A king needs a queen," she said, her breath warm against his cheek.

He pulled back hastily. Those words had been too enticing to him. But when he inspected her face, it wasn't altered. She wasn't using her Affinity; she simply *was* what he desired—exactly what he desired.

Maybe revenge was unnecessary. Maybe, in appeasing himself, he could appease her, too.

"All right, Belven." He disentangled his hands to take a step away. "What's your plan?"

A smirk crept onto her lips. "You're willing to work together?"

He never had been. In juvie he'd been a loner, by choice and not by choice. If Hastings hadn't abused him from the start, maybe they would have been allies. Nero had never bothered to open himself up to the idea. But Orla...she was powerful in a way that would compliment him. They would make a formidable pair.

"Depends on the plan."

She relaxed at that, a display of confidence that sent a wave of giddiness through Nero. "Avner and his friends are hosting an event tonight—JAMZ. It's basically a fight club. You'll have to participate."

A malicious grin cracked onto Nero's lips. "I don't think *have to* is the right word choice."

"You'll have to challenge Mensen."

"The blind girl? You want me to beat up a blind girl?"

"Well, you don't stand a chance against Avner."

Nero bristled, appalled. "I *do*—"

"It doesn't matter," she dismissed, waving a hand. "Avner will recover from his own beating. He won't recover from

Zeela's. It'll crush him, and he's too good-natured to retaliate. Or maybe you could just disfigure her face enough that he breaks up with her in disgust."

"Why? So you can swoop in and bang him?"

"*No*, so we can dismantle their group. The four of them—Avner, Zeela, Jamad, Maddy—they're too strong, and...they rule this place. Everyone respects them; everyone likes them."

"I'm sensing a feud," Nero said, not at all displeased.

"It...doesn't matter..."

"It does matter." He puffed his chest and crossed his arms. "I want to know the history here—and *your* history. Tell me how you got your Affinity."

He expected her to squirm, but her tone was steely as she said, "Why does it matter to you?"

"I'm *interested*," he answered, roving her face for any sign of weakness.

There was a moment of strained silence before she tonelessly said, "I was born with brown hair."

He hadn't anticipated she'd say anything, least of all that. "So?"

"So, my mother wanted a blonde. She was blonde as a child, and she was disappointed that my features were so dark. She called me ugly—and I felt ugly—and therefore I *was* ugly. She...always favored my younger sister because of it— because Kiki was blonde. It was the stupidest thing, and it probably wasn't as exaggerated as I perceived it, but...it was enough."

Spite flared in Orla's eyes, so akin to Nero's own that he almost touched her again—not as some rough statement of power, but as affectionate consolation. He knew too well what it was like to be a parent's disappointment, to be the least favored.

"And your Affinity gave you what your mother wanted." Just as his Affinity had given him what his father wanted: a strong, tough son who was capable of enduring all his labors.

Orla jolted forward, like she might attack him. "What *I* wanted. You don't think I relish this ability?"

He knew she did because, even though Miller had been the cause of his Affinity, Nero still thrived in it.

"I think...you don't need it," he concluded, lifting her chin toward his. "Not with me, anyway."

"I do need it *for* us," she said softly. "I'll need to distract Avner and Jamad while you fight Zeela. Otherwise, they'll intervene."

"Jamad—the frosty-haired kid?" Orla nodded, and he dropped his finger from her chin with a snort. "That kid seemed like he liked you just fine without your Affinity."

Her lips slid into a lopsided smirk. "He has a bit of a crush, yeah."

"Well, then I hope you don't mind if I crush *him*."

Orla let out a laugh that was more of a cackle. "Not at all."

"When is this fight club?"

"Midnight."

"Then this is the last day it'll be known as *JAMZ*. After tonight, it'll be our dominion. And until then...what are your plans?" he asked, trailing a finger up her throat.

Although he knew she didn't, his body could have sworn she turned on her Affinity as she leaned in to breathe, "I think you know."

Even though Nero spent the entirety of that Friday afternoon with Orla, they didn't walk to JAMZ together. They couldn't be seen as allies—not yet. Instead, he found himself trekking from the Residence Tower to the Physicals Building with Ruse at his side.

"So, you ended up being interested after all, huh?" the kid mused, surveying Nero's disheveled hair. He could have claimed it was bed-head, but then Ruse motioned to his cheek, and when Nero swiped at his own, he found Orla's pink lipstick smeared on his hand.

"Yeah," he admitted, smirking mildly at the thought. When Ruse snickered, Nero's demeanor hardened. "Bet you wouldn't know anything about it."

"About what? A girl's body?" he challenged as his features began to change. In horror, Nero watched Ruse's boyish form morph into that of a woman, his unappealing face turning into something almost *beautiful*. A watered-down version of Orla, with hair like bronze rather than gold.

"Dammit," the boy—now girl—muttered, glaring down at his chest. "I can never get the boobs right. They're always uneven—and *heavy...*"

"Maybe you're just weak," Nero said with a snort. After watching Ruse shift back into his previous form—male body, brown hair, hazel eyes, pale skin—he gruffly added, "You are...talented, though. I could use you."

Ruse shifted a few steps away from Nero, nearly bumping into a group of girls walking along the path. "Use me how?" he questioned warily.

Grabbing his arm, Nero yanked Ruse back to his side effortlessly. "I need you to distract that girl during JAMZ—Maddy."

"Martinez? The stretchy one? But...why?"

"You'll see," he growled, violently releasing Ruse's arm.

Rubbing himself like a wounded puppy, the boy said, "That sounds ominous. I'm not sure I want any part in your schemes."

A low rumble escaped Nero's throat, but threatening Ruse would get him nowhere. For some reason, this kid was immune to his intimidation. "Are you implying you're incapable?"

That piqued his attention. "*No.* Of course I'm capable…" He trailed off, eyeing Nero in a way that implied he knew exactly what the brute was up to. Still, there was a keenness in his eyes, a determination to prove himself. "I'll do it—but only because I think Maddy's cool and I'd enjoy having a conversation with her. It has nothing to do with you."

"Right," Nero said, almost amused when Ruse skipped ahead. As he weaved through the crowd, his body transformed until he was indistinguishable.

Feeling content with his charisma, Nero was prepared to walk the rest of the way alone, another body in the river of students milling across campus. After passing through the glass doors into the Physicals Building, however, he emerged in the white-walled hallway with a new companion at his side.

"You seem smug," Jerry noted, pink-streaked eyes trained on the bobbing heads before them.

"I'm sure you know exactly why."

"You're not as easy to read as you think. You've got walls around your mind, walls even you can't penetrate."

Nero didn't like hearing that. Even if he wasn't easy to read, he didn't want Jerry knowing about his self-imposed mental blocks.

Of course, Jerry probably knew that, which was why he'd pointed it out.

"Emotions are for weaklings," Nero said as they passed the gymnasium doors, propped open to reveal the desolate and dark room where he often unleashed his emotions through aggression. This week alone he'd sent three kids to the nurse's office during training.

Maybe emotions can draw out strength, too, he thought, since he couldn't bear to admit the words aloud.

Sometimes too much strength, Jerry added, likely referring to the fiasco with Nero's half-siblings, which weighed heavily on his mind. He didn't feel guilt, but there was regret. If he hadn't let his emotions control him, he wouldn't have spent three years of his life in juvie.

"My emotions have gotten me into shit, too," Jerry said with his physical voice. "You saw that yourself."

Nero wasn't sure if the image came to his mind naturally or if Jerry planted it there, but he vividly recalled the beating he'd walked in on. "With…your dad?" Nero clarified, hating the way the word sounded on his tongue—*dad*.

"Yeah, that asshole." Jerry shot him a wry glance, knowing he could relate, as they followed the crowd into a narrow stairwell. *He's always resented me because I remind him of my mother—who left him to pursue an actual career and dumped me on him,* Jerry thought. His voice would have echoed here, and Nero understood his desire not to be heard. *I'd probably resent me, too. I read him well enough to sympathize…until I realized what a lowlife he is.*

"I wish I could call my dad a lowlife," Nero grumbled, receiving a puzzled look from the boy in front of them. Switching to his mental voice, he added, *He's an upstanding citizen, and that I hate him makes me seem like the douche. That guy's always been a prick to me.*

I know the feeling, Jerry thought, reminding Nero of why

the mind reader was the only person here he'd taken a liking to. *He's always thought I'm a disappointment. I've never cared about his opinion, but as you saw, he has a temper. My Affinity formed because I always needed to know what he was thinking, if he was drawing near—and then warn others silently.*

Nero's brow creased slightly. *Others?*

Jerry refused to look at him, keeping his eyes blankly ahead, as they landed on the basement floor. *I had a... significant other. We weren't official, but...I couldn't stop him from sneaking over to see me. My dad didn't approve, since he approves of nothing I do, so I had to keep it a secret. He caught us together last week, just before you arrived. That was why he was beating me.*

A strange sensation tugged at Nero's chest, and he struggled to swallow as they entered a vast warehouse-like room where students congregated. He'd never been claustrophobic, but Jerry's story had disturbed him, and perhaps hit a spot in his own mind that was too raw for comfort. The prospect of spending the next few hours in this room full of people, engaging in violence...it suddenly sickened him.

Dazed, he scanned the ring of students forming around a square of orange mats. When his eyes fixed on a head of metallic hair glittering in the dim lighting, his brain snapped back into its natural state of heartlessness. He had an ally, a plan, a goal. No sob story would deflect him from his path.

"I don't expect to change you," Jerry began, his voice startling Nero with its coolness. "I've tried with too many people, and it never works. Just know you're not the only one who's dealt with adversity."

Nero glared at him from the corner of his eye. "I know that."

"Not as well as you should." The words sounded more

like a warning than a reprimand.

"What—"

"Good evening, everyone." Avner Stromer's feeble voice barely carried over the chatter, but everyone shut up anyway. Maybe it was a little unfair of Nero to call Avner *feeble*. Stromer was definitely broader than Dave or Jerry, and he exuded a reasonable amount of confidence for a sixteen-year-old. Still, he glowed with kindness, which disgusted Nero almost as much as the putrid color of his hair.

"Welcome to JAMZ," Avner said into the quiet chamber. "My friends and I formed this event last year after seeing how strict the teachers—"

"Namely Fraco," the frosty-haired kid, Jamad, chirped, earning a bout of chuckles.

"—are during training," Avner finished, a fresh grin on his lips. "Now, that doesn't mean this is a dangerous, lawless event. There are some rules, which I'll go over…"

And that was Nero's cue to stop listening. *Rules* were not a part of the plan, and he wouldn't let them hinder him.

"This is pretty cool, huh?" a feminine voice whispered, and Nero pivoted to find that Jia had materialized beside him. Her raisin purple eyes brimmed with awe. "It feels like we're in a speakeasy during the Prohibition."

"A what in the what?" Nero questioned, wrinkling his nose.

"They really didn't teach you U.S. history in juvie? That should be a crime—but I guess it makes sense that they wouldn't want to discuss the semi-successful illicit acts of the past with a group of kids who are primed to engage in similarly illegal activity…"

"Any volunteers for the first brawl?" Avner asked as Jia continued to jabber about history. Without hesitation, Nero grabbed her shoulders and thrust her onto the mats.

"Ow, what the—" Stumbling and nearly slamming into Avner, Jia managed to right herself, straightening her posture as she gazed at the crowd surrounding her.

"Oh…kay," Avner said with uncertainty. Squinting, he searched the crowd for the source of Jia's unexpected emergence, but in a half-crouch, Nero remained inconspicuous. "Well…does anyone wanna challenge her?"

"I will," a boy volunteered as he stepped onto the mats. Slight and spindly, he looked like a life-sized feather-duster with his crazy, ash-gray locks sprouting from his gourd-shaped head.

Avner winced. "You can't suffocate her, Hazy. You know this."

"Of course," the boy said in a voice as elusive as smoke. His strides were fluid, prowling toward Jia with predatory ease, and Nero probably should have felt bad about throwing her in the ring with such a creep, but he didn't. The plan had never been for Nero to challenge Zeela forthright. He couldn't seem too eager; he had to allow Orla a few rounds to work her charm, to entrance Avner and Jamad enough that they couldn't intervene.

Luckily, she was already at it. Jamad had settled beside her, head tilted as he listened to her whispered words. Avner, probably to disentangle his friend, approached the pair, but as soon as Orla met his eyes, his purpose dwindled into mindlessness.

Maybe Nero would only have to wait one round to use his fists.

The boy named Hazy circled Jia now, jumping his eyebrows rhythmically. Biting her lip, she seemed a bit nervous—or maybe disturbed—but it wasn't enough to paralyze her into defenselessness. As soon as Hazy lifted his hands, dark smoke curling at his fingertips, she squeezed her eyes shut, and then, as if blowing her nose, she snorted.

Nero thought it was a sneeze until a deluge of color spurted from Jia's nose, exploding toward Hazy in an aggressive rainbow. For a surreal moment, Nero almost believed she had some kind of magical rainbow Affinity, but pieces of the rainbow projected into the crowd, and when he bent to pick up a few at his feet, he saw they were little plastic beads, like a child might use to make a bracelet.

It should have been a pathetic Affinity, but the force of Jia's snort hurdled the beads at Hazy with such speed that he staggered backward, clutching his stomach from the blow.

The entire audience was stunned. Nero had definitely not expected that from Jia. Judging by what he knew of the girl so far, he'd assumed she had an Affinity for knowing history facts no one else cared about. But as it turned out, she was *powerful*—powerful enough that he wouldn't have minded her as an ally.

"Did you know?" he asked Jerry, who seemed unfazed.

"No. All she ever thinks about is history."

"Figures..." Nero muttered, setting his eyes back on the brawl. Hazy hadn't stumbled enough to fall off the mats, but Jia's attack had enraged him. With slivered eyes, he advanced on her like a human-shaped candle wick, smoke seeping from every pore. She ran around in circles to avoiding him, periodically shooting a few beads in his direction.

"The snorting gives her a headache," Jerry explained, probably having read her thoughts.

"And she can't...project the beads any other way?" Nero asked.

"Apparently not..." Jerry's voice fizzled out as his vision

fixed beyond the mats, where the founders of JAMZ were positioned.

Orla still had the boys enraptured with soft words and batting eyelashes, but Zeela and Maddy were oblivious to it. Mensen's snow-white eyes watched Jia and Hazy as if she could *see* them, and Nero wondered, with a flicker of apprehension, if she actually could. Orla had never said *what* the blind girl's Affinity was. What if she had the ability to predict Nero's movements with those ominous eyes? What if she managed to *beat* him in their fight?

The notion was ludicrous. He had domineered an entire facility of delinquents; one blind girl wouldn't thwart him. Thinking about it wasn't smart, though. If Jerry could read minds, perhaps others could, as well. He tried to throw walls around his brain, and he was about to ask Jerry if it was working, but then he noticed the mind reader had gone rigid.

Tentatively curious, Nero followed his gaze again. It still rested in the direction of the JAMZ founders, but the object of his focus was Maddy—or rather, the person talking to Maddy.

Nero knew it was Ruse. The tall boy with blond hair and pale eyes looked too much like a Regg to belong in Periculand. Plus, the features of his face—angular jaw, fine nose, sly lips—were too perfect to be natural. Only a shapeshifter could produce such perfection. Nero had to give him credit for distracting Maddy so thoroughly.

Jerry was oddly distracted, as well. His mouth drooped wider than usual, and Nero thought maybe he was merely ogling Ruse's uncanny good looks, but there was a hint of bewilderment in his expression.

"What?" Nero asked, elbowing him lightly. Jerry didn't flinch.

"That's…*him*."

"Dispus? Yeah, I told him to…" Nero stopped talking when Jerry's horror intensified. He had to grab hold of Nero's arm to steady himself, and even then he wobbled. If he were anyone else, Nero would have shoved him off, but he liked Jerry. And Jerry, it appeared, had broken.

"It's—*no*—I-I didn't… I didn't recognize…"

The realization dawned on Nero with piercing clarity. "You—you and *Dispus*? You were with *Dispus*? *He* was your significant other?"

"I didn't—he told me his name was *Sheldon*," Jerry half-choked, half-moaned.

"Well, you should have known *that* was a lie. There's no way in hell a guy like that would be named *Sheldon*."

"I didn't recognize his mind—how did I not recognize his mind?" Jerry swayed and Nero easily righted him.

"Do you…recognize it now?"

"Y-yes. His brashness, his wildness, his…softness—"

Nero gagged. "Let's not get sappy here, Watkins. You're positive it was Dispus you were banging?"

"Positive. God, this is embarrassing. We were *serious*, and he had to have recognized me as soon as he got into the van, but he didn't say anything, and he *hasn't* said anything…"

"No, he hasn't," Nero agreed darkly, his glower now trained on Ruse. "He's been purposely ignoring you—after he abandoned you to get beaten by your father."

For once, Jerry clamped his lips shut, saying and thinking nothing. That was how Nero knew he had been given permission. In his slowly simmering rage, his brain was an open book, and he was thinking very intricately about what he wished to do to Ruse. The mind reader knew, and he wasn't opposed.

Removing Jerry's arm from his was the last gentle movement he engaged in. After that, he didn't care who he touched—who he hurt—as he barreled through the crowd and onto the mats, into the acrid fog of Hazy's smoke.

Jia—still running around in circles, now sneezing *and* coughing—was the first person Nero encountered, and he tripped her by the ankle before ramming Hazy with his shoulder.

He felt the reverberations of their falls right before he plunged off the mats and into the crowd on the opposite side. Zeela stood there, only a few measly feet from him, but in his vision she was an inconsequential blur of white. Not a finger was laid on her.

Nero had no qualms with laying all his fingers on Ruse, though—viciously.

"Whoa!" the shapeshifter exclaimed as Nero tackled him to the concrete. There were no mats to lessen the blow of the fall, but Ruse was smart enough to rotate, saving his head by giving his shoulder the brunt of the impact.

The crack of his bones sunk into Nero's ears like a drug. Screw Ruse. No matter how much potential his power offered, he was worthless, and soon he would be pulp.

"Nero!" Orla called from afar, but he didn't even look at her. "What are you doing?"

"Yeah, what are you doing?" Ruse hissed, grimacing beneath Nero's weight. "I was doing what you asked—"

"I never asked you to lie to Jerry," he growled, and the boy's eyes snapped open in alarm. They were that pukey greenish gray now, hideous enough to encompass his personality. "I never asked you to abandon Jerry so his father could punish him. You didn't even try to help him, you little *bitch*."

"He told me to run!"

"Yeah, and he was being noble. You aren't; you let the one you love get hurt—"

His ragged breaths caught at the end as he listened to his own words. Nero had avoided thinking about it for years, but he had, essentially, allowed the one he loved to get hurt, too. In his fifteen years of life, his mother had been the only person he ever loved, and *he* had abandoned her—he'd gotten himself thrown in juvie, breaking her heart.

He was as bad as Ruse—maybe worse.

"I thought it was just a fling—a hook up thing," Ruse grunted, wiggling beneath Nero's clutches. "We were just having fun—I didn't wanna get *beaten!*"

"Well," Nero said through a callous laugh, "now you will."

Shouts rang through the air, but Nero was numb to them. His primal instincts had kicked in, and he pummeled Ruse relentlessly, punching and punching and punching, hoping his brains would spill out of his skull.

There was a point when he heard Jerry's mental voice— *Stop... STOP*—but it wasn't until a spark of electricity coursed through him, incapacitating his muscles, that he finally flopped to the side, staring up at the fluorescent lights in a euphoric stupor.

Ruse had gotten what he deserved, for now.

6

The Cycle of Pain

Through his swollen eyelids, Ruse could barely see Avner Stromer looming above him, hand over his mouth with worry. The lighting was brighter here than it had been in the JAMZ basement, but Ruse wasn't entirely sure where *here* was.

"I still don't understand how this could have happened," a man's voice said, wrought with concern. "The skull...the nose...the *blood*..."

"Maybe you should heal him first, then he can explain," Jamad advised, shifting beside Avner. His hazy vision didn't give him much detail, but Ruse discerned a few scratches on Jamad's dark skin that hadn't been there before.

"Right..." the man muttered, and then Ruse felt a finger on his temple. He jolted at the touch, at the rawness of his flesh, but slowly, it subsided. The pain muddying his thoughts and clouding his vision drifted away, giving him clarity. They were in the nurse's office and Jason Pane stood beside him in orange scrubs, hand pressed to Ruse's forehead. His eyes and hair were the same color as the bruises on Ruse's arms—the bruises that were vanishing.

"You all right?" Avner asked, lowering his hand to his side.

Ruse nodded, and it didn't give him a headache. "Uh, yeah…I'm good."

"What happened to you?" the nurse asked, retreating a step from the white bed Ruse lounged upon.

"I…fell down the stairs," he lied. Nero was an ass for what he'd done, but Ruse wouldn't tattle. Adults had never solved his problems for him. In all honesty, Lavisa had usually been the one to stick up for him in physical matters, but here, he was on his own. Luckily, he was slippery enough to wheedle his way out of situations—most, at least.

"The black eyes…" the nurse began tentatively, "seemed more like punch-inflicted wounds."

"Nah, I think my eyes just…hit the railing…or maybe my own fists as I fell," Ruse assured him. Avner and Jamad couldn't even pretend to look convinced by that. "It's not a big deal. Thanks for healing—"

"What is going on here!" With that exclamation, Fraco Leve burst into the nurse's office, clothed in his oily suit, his typical clipboard notably absent. "Students out of bed after curfew, getting injured—"

"I fell down the stairs," Ruse repeated, trying to sound more earnest. "I was…out of my room after curfew, yeah. I wanted to hang out with Avner and Jamad, 'cus they're cool and older, but then I must've been so sleepy I tripped down the stairs."

Fraco's eyes narrowed, two slits of gleaming darkness. "I would like to believe you, Mr. Dispus, but this is not the first time students have ended up in the nurse's office after curfew with Mr. Stromer and Mr. Solberg accompanying them."

"We're just *that* cool, Fraco." Jamad wiggled his eyebrows. "Everyone wants to hang out with us after curfew…and then fall down the stairs afterward."

The man's nose twitched like an angry rabbit's. "It's *Mr. Leve—*"

"I don't want to cause any problems," the nurse said, glancing between the boys with an apologetic look, "but if those wounds were inflicted by another student, we must know. We can't allow this level of violence to go unpunished."

"You believe it was another student?" Fraco squeaked in disbelief. "Then this is serious!"

"It...was," Jamad admitted, exchanging an uneasy glance with Avner.

To Ruse's surprise, Avner didn't panic about the prospect of his friend revealing JAMZ. Ruse was freaking out, though, because if they told on Nero, the brute would know, and he would seek revenge.

"It happened in the tower," Jamad said. "Another student was pissed at Ruse for...personal reasons."

"Well, who was it?" Fraco prompted.

Ruse shook his head ever so slightly, but Avner either didn't see or blatantly ignored him, because, with an awkward cough, he said, "It was Nero."

"Nero Corvis?" Fraco blinked, not with shock but with trepidation. "Oh, well, this is not good... Mr. Periculy knew it would be dangerous to bring him here, but...this..."

"It was provoked," Ruse said, which wasn't *totally* a lie. He'd been a downright douche, and he knew it. Ditching Jerry had been bad enough, but to keep his identity a secret from him in the van... He did deserve that beating.

Part of him hadn't been ready to admit how much he actually cared for Jerry, especially after he'd abandoned him, earning the other boy's eternal hatred. He was also an idiot for morphing into that form, the form Jerry had fallen for. It *was* the most attractive appearance he'd ever assumed, though, and he'd wanted to impress Nero with his abilities. His cowardice, his groveling…it had all earned him this.

"No matter the circumstances, violence is prohibited amongst students," Fraco declared, and Ruse knew nothing he said would sway the man's mind. "I must report to Mr. Periculy, but first, I will escort you boys back to the tower. Frankly, you should be punished as well, Mr. Dispus, for being stupid enough to provoke Mr. Corvis. It's no secret where he's spent the last three years."

"Yeah, punish me," Ruse encouraged. "Nero and I can get a joint punishing. It'll…bond us, or something."

Fraco pursed his lips dubiously. "I will have to decline that one, Mr. Dispus. Now, let's head back to the—"

"We can walk ourselves back to the tower, Mr. Leve," Avner said smoothly, probably thinking that the vice principal would notice all of the students absent from the tower if he went anywhere near it. "You shouldn't waste any time before reporting to Mr. Periculy. Nero could be…plotting how to injure other students."

"You're right," Fraco said reluctantly. "I shall report to Mr. Periculy and then retrieve Mr. Corvis immediately. I advise returning to your rooms before I do so."

Thankfully, he didn't stick around to see if they'd listened. Once he'd departed, Avner and Jamad waited a painful minute before exiting the nurse's office. Ruse hopped off the table, giving the nurse a wave, and followed them into the hallway. They practically ran.

"We need to get everyone out of the basement and back to their rooms before Fraco gets to the tower!"

"And you can't come," Jamad added to Ruse before they entered the stairwell.

"But—"

"If Nero sees you—and that you're *healed*—he'll throw a fit. We need him as compliant as possible unless we all wanna get in a shit-ton of trouble. *Go.*"

Ruse wanted to argue that he could make himself look like anyone, but…Nero would always know it was him, because Jerry would always know it was him. Now that the mind reader was aware of Ruse's presence at this school, he would always recognize his consciousness. They'd spent too much time conversing through their minds for him not to. It disappointed Ruse, really, that it had taken Jerry this long to realize… But that was stupid. He'd concealed himself, and he'd never told the other boy the whole truth of his abilities—or even that he was an Affinity.

He was a liar, a trickster, a ruse, and he didn't deserve Jerry.

Trudging back to the tower, he wished the beating had been worse.

Disoriented by his lingering fury, Nero didn't fully process what was happening when he returned to his dormitory, only to be summoned minutes later by the probably-pedophile Aethelred.

For a pedophile, the red-haired man was awfully careful not to touch Nero in any fashion as he ushered him from room 206 to the lounge and then out of the Residence Tower completely. It wasn't until they walked on the path from the tower to the Mentals Building, cloaked in near-darkness, that the man spoke.

"Were you imagining Ruse was one of your half-siblings?" he asked, staring pensively at the night sky.

Nero was so taken aback by the forwardness of his question that he nearly balked. "*No.* Don't try to dissect my brain like some creepy therapist. There were no *hidden motives* behind it. Dispus was a dick, so I tried to destroy him. If Stromer hadn't intervened, I would have done this world a service."

"May I ask what Mr. Dispus did to offend you?"

"It's not your business," he said with a new sense of calmness. It must have stemmed from the realization that Aethelred knew what had happened, even though he hadn't been there, which meant... "Dispus *tattled* on me, didn't he? That little mole—"

"From what I've gathered, it wasn't a willing tattling. Fraco can be very persuasive."

Aethelred's tone was whimsical, but Nero found nothing humorous about this. Dispus had ratted him out, and now he would receive some type of punishment...in the Mentals Building.

"Where are you taking me?" he demanded, at which the man gave him a sympathetic look.

"I'm sorry, Nero. I'd rather not do this, but Mr. Periculy has requested that I bring you to his office." His pitying gaze turned apologetic as he swung open the glass door. Nero felt too numb to do anything other than trudge into the library. The last time he'd been in here had been with Orla, when his plans of domination had formed. Now those plans were crumbling around him because of *Ruse.*

"Is he gonna expel me?" Nero asked, unsure of how he felt about the prospect. Despite his feuds here, Periculand was preferable to juvie.

"No, he won't expel you," Aethelred assured, but it didn't

sound very consoling. Nero remembered the first and only time he'd ever met Mr. Periculy, and he acknowledged there could be worse punishments than returning to juvie.

After ascending the stairs in silence, they arrived at the long, empty corridor of the fourth floor. Halfway down rested a pair of white doors, which yawned open at their approach, exposing the grandeur of Periculy's office.

The entire room was drenched in red: red wood floors, red-painted walls, red armchairs before the grand desk. Beyond it, Periculy sat in a swivel chair, his back to the glass wall, a sheet of black to reflect the night. His presence swallowed the other details of the room. Despite the might of his strength Affinity, Nero hesitated in the doorway.

"Mr. Corvis," the principal greeted, a faint smile on his lips. "It's been quite some time since we last met. You may leave us, Aethelred."

Dipping his chin, the man gave Nero one last indecipherable look before retreating to the stairwell. Alone, Nero stepped into the office, fighting to keep his head high.

Periculy gestured toward the armchairs. "Have a seat."

Nero convinced himself he had a choice as he slumped into the one on the left. It was a tight fit, but the chair instilled the least of his discomfort.

"I see your years in the detention center have treated you well." Periculy inclined his head, and Nero knew he was referring to his super strength. "Intimidation is in your DNA. The need for domination is, as well. I always wondered, with you and Hastings in a room together, who would emerge victorious. I've heard it was Hastings."

Nero's fists clenched atop the armrests. "I never touched that kid. He had it easy. I would have had no problem pummeling him as much as I pummeled Ruse."

"Ah, so you aren't going to deny it? Interesting. Most students would play innocent."

"You must have this whole town rigged with cameras," Nero scoffed, eyeing the walls and ceiling, searching for one. "You are the god of this place, after all."

There was a flicker of fascination in Periculy's pink eyes. "Perceptive. I do know exactly what you did to Ruse Dispus, and I would have known even if Fraco hadn't forced the truth. Now I'm curious as to what Ruse did to provoke you. He claims he did."

"Yeah," Nero said through gritted teeth, "well, I'm curious as to what your connection to Hastings is. Why is he your golden boy over anyone else?"

"Oh, I'm aware you dislike him, Nero, but the boy has had a tough life. Left to his own devices, he would become a...monster." Periculy paused, and Nero saw the realization on his face—the realization that Nero had become the very monster this man feared. Probably because this douche had never extended his hospitality to him.

Regaining his composure, the principal continued. "Hastings will come to Periculand in two years, and I want him as obedient as possible. And, of course, obedience is the issue for which you are here. Not many students ever see me," he said, standing from his chair to stroll around his desk. "Student involvement is not normally my responsibility, but with violence of this severity...I'm forced to intervene. I gather you're not the kind of person who takes small punishments to heart."

Nero swallowed as casually as he could. Periculy sat at on the edge his desk now, eyeing the boy like an experiment.

"Dispus deserved what he got," Nero huffed. "I'm sure he won't do it again."

"You can't be sure, though; you can never be sure of anyone else's actions, only your own."

"Fine," Nero ground out, clutching the armrests. "*I* won't do it again."

"We'll ensure you don't." Periculy stood again, towering over Nero. He wouldn't have if the boy stood, as well, but he'd been cornered into this chair. Only brute strength might save him, but Nero had a feeling Periculy would have no problem resisting a physical attack. The man wore a purple suit, as he had three years ago, and Nero now knew what that meant: Mental.

"Mr. Pane evaded telling me of the exact injuries you inflicted on Ruse Dispus, but I saw: a broken nose, a fractured skull, bruises everywhere. Have you ever experienced any of those?"

"Bruises everywhere?" Nero repeated roughly. "Why don't you ask your little apprentice about that?"

"Hastings has been practicing his Affinity in a nonlethal way, as all Affinities are encouraged to do. Did you ever notice those bruises healed quicker than they should have?"

Nero *had* noticed, but he didn't want to admit it.

"That was Hastings's doing, as well. He can injure, and he can heal. You and he are similar in that way. You have the ability to destroy, Nero, but also the ability to build. Strength and power are not evil—"

"But I am?" he challenged, feeling his fingers break through the fabric of the armrest. Periculy either didn't notice or didn't care.

"No, you aren't evil. You've simply never been disciplined."

"You don't know anything about me," Nero snapped, bolting from his chair as thoughts of *Miller* clouded his mind.

His chest heaved a few inches from Periculy's face, but the man didn't seem alarmed.

"I know all about your father," he said softly but not kindly, "and I do pity you. But you must know you don't hold all authority everywhere he's not. You need to see past yourself—see that everyone struggles.

"This will be a lesson in empathy, Nero. Not many can hurt you, but you can hurt many. It's time you understand the pain others experience when you hit them. I will let you choose, though. Since you already know all about bruises, would you prefer a fractured nose or a fractured skull first?"

Slumped on his bed, Nero was rubbing his nose and head when a knock sounded on the door. The night had passed, and Dave was out somewhere this morning—probably with freaking *Ruse*. Nero knew it wasn't his roommate at the door; the knock itself was too dainty—girlish. That's why he wasn't the least bit surprised when the knob turned and Orla materialized in the doorway.

Clothed in a mini-skirt and a flattering crop-top, she looked as attractive as always, permeating his thoughts with her presence. Her golden eyes were harsher than usual, though—less dazzling. With all that had unfolded the night before, he'd nearly forgotten she had reason to be angry with him.

"What do you want?" he grumbled, staring at the ground.

She took a step toward him, and he sensed her hesitancy. Whatever indignation she'd harbored clearly mollified at the sight of his hunched shoulders and sullen mood.

"Are you okay?" she asked with genuine concern. "Did

Periculy…punish you?"

"No, I'm just feeling inconsolably guilty because I hurt precious little Ruse."

Unfortunately, his biting sarcasm didn't prompt her to storm out of the room; instead, she slunk toward him until he felt her plop on the bed beside him. Still, he refused to glance in her direction.

"You seem lucid enough to conjure words like *inconsolably*."

"Yeah, and you seem like you're trying to comfort me but have no clue how."

"I've…never had friends to comfort before," she admitted, and there was a rawness to her tone that made Nero finally pivot his head. The empathy in her expression was far greater than the empathy he had been instructed to feel when Periculy tortured him a few hours ago. "I'm trying not to use my Affinity on you. It makes our…alliance feel fake, and I don't want that."

"Alliance," Nero snorted, shaking his head. "You were gonna say *friendship*, weren't you?"

"No…I was gonna say relationship."

Slowly, his narrowed eyes slid toward her. "It's been a week, Belven."

"I know." She sighed, and for the first time he could recall, her posture waned. "But we have a connection, don't we? You're the first person who really gets me—who sees this place with the same eyes. A week was enough for you to start loathing Ruse Dispus. Hasn't it been enough for you to start…liking me, at least a little?"

"Dispus did something to make me loathe him. What have you done to make me like you?" It was a heartless statement, and Nero knew it, but Orla had a heart of metal, even stronger than gold, and she didn't flinch at the insult.

"I'm here with you now, aren't I?" she questioned in little more than a whisper.

Nero felt her inching closer to him, their arms now millimeters from each other. Part of him wanted to lean into her, not because she provoked him with her Affinity or even because she was attractive, but because he wanted a companion—a relationship—something real, like she'd said.

"After what you did last night, I'm the only one here"— she brushed her hand against his clenched fist—"the only one who isn't afraid of you, the only one who believes in you...the only one who spoke in your favor at breakfast this morning."

Jolting upright, Nero stood to glare down at her. "What happened at breakfast this morning?"

Though she fidgeted on his bed, her elegant posture had resumed. "Fraco announced that curfew will be more strictly enforced from now on. He didn't say *how* he would do so, but students were riotous regardless. They all started blaming you, and Jamad told people you'd be banned from all future JAMZ sessions. Everyone seemed ready to march up here as a mob and attack you, but I made them see reason, as much as I could."

With the weariness in her expression, Nero wondered if part of the reason she didn't use her Affinity on him now was because attempting to wield it against an entire cafeteria had depleted her.

"So," he said as he paced throughout his room, "Fraco's not gonna enforce the curfew?"

Orla winced slightly. "Fraco is difficult for me to woo. He doesn't seem very attracted to women—or men—or anyone other than Periculy. I'm convinced he would die for his principal."

"Then maybe I need to have another chat with Periculy..."

"Nero," she interjected carefully, "is that really necessary?"

"How am I supposed to gain this school's respect if they all hate me because of some stupid curfew?"

"Doesn't... I mean... There have been rumors...but doesn't Periculy... Didn't he torture you?"

Nero's pacing halted, his vicious attention settling acutely on Orla. "No one is capable of torturing me."

She bit her lip, eyeing him with sympathy. "It's okay to talk about it. I won't think any less of—"

"*No one* is capable of torturing me," he repeated forcefully. "No one can hurt me, and no one can sway my decisions, not even you."

"Nero," she implored, standing to face him directly. Even on her feet, she was a head shorter than him, but she tilted her face toward him, close enough to plant a kiss if she chose to. "I don't want to make your decisions—I don't want to control you. I want you to control yourself. Think rationally. This is not a physical game we're playing. This is *mental*. Violence won't solve everything."

"Violence will solve everything," he countered, enunciating each word. Then, before he could think to stop himself, his fingers were clamped around her neck, encasing her delicate skin in the coarseness of his.

Her eyes protruded like two golden coins, and her perfect lips parted, hoping to inhale air. She couldn't. Nero's grip was too tight, and a distant part of his brain knew he was strangling her, but the primal, wrathful side of him had taken hold.

"Violence is what stopped my visits to douche-bag Miller's. Violence is what prevented me from becoming the bitch in juvie. Violence is what saved Jerry from his dick of a father, and it's what'll save him from that asswipe Dispus—"

Nero.

The voice was strong in his brain, diffusing into every crevice. It didn't force him to drop Orla, but it persuaded him to.

Grip slackening, Nero staggered back, and she toppled onto his bed, heaving for breath, clutching her own throat as if to ensure that it still functioned. She stared at him, wide-eyed, and he realized the weight of what he'd done. The one person who had trusted him, who had placed her faith in him—he'd almost killed her. Once again, his anger had led to an irrevocable mistake, disproving his pro-violence argument completely.

"I-I'm sorry," he choked, the words sounding foreign on his tongue. He was almost certain he'd never said them before. "I didn't mean—"

"It's fine," she interrupted, standing once more to straighten her rumpled clothing. "I'm fine. I don't want to talk about this again. Let's just move on and decide how to best deal with the situation unfolding in this school."

"I—okay," he said, because he was too embarrassed and shaken by his own actions to say much else. She sat upon his bed again—legs crossed, formal and aloof—to discuss their plan. As partners but not as *partners*. As allies but nothing more.

Nero processed her words but barely heard her voice. All he could think of were the sounds of her choking in his grasp. He really would have done it, too; his festering rage really would have consumed him enough to murder, and then he would have gone back to juvie. He would have doomed himself— if not for the boy lingering in the hallway, whose pink head of hair swept by the open doorway as Orla hashed out her plans for power.

7

A Death Wish

Avner would never admit it, but the JAMZ session had shaken him. They'd had a few problems upon starting the club in their first year, but nothing like Nero. This kid was a whole new breed of problematic.

It was clear he wanted authority, and his method of acquiring authority was violence. Throughout dinner that evening, he'd glared at Avner as if debating which form of execution would fit him best. Avner didn't fear for his own safety—or even Jamad's or Maddy's—but Zeela... She was smart and tough, but physical defense had never been her strength.

That was why he'd decided he and Jamad would sleep in the girls' room until they were certain Nero had no plans to attack in the middle of the night. He'd left dinner early to trek up to the fifth floor of the Residence Tower and move his essentials to Zeela's room, but he barely made it to the second floor before his path was impeded.

"Avner," a cringe-invoking voice cooed. He didn't have to see the shimmer of gold to know who it was.

"Orla," he greeted stiffly, attempting to sidestep her on the second floor landing. She barred his path by placing her hands on either railing, trapping him on the stairs.

"Normally I wouldn't bother talking to you, but I heard a girl crying in that room over there." She pointed her manicured finger toward the open door of room 204. From this angle, it looked vacant. "I'm worried she might be hurt."

Avner's expression remained flat. "And you didn't bother to check on her?"

"I don't have a kind-hearted nature. I would call her pathetic if I went in there on my own. But you—you're like my moral compass, Av. If you come with me, I'm sure we can cheer her up."

Nose wrinkling at the thought of being Orla's compass—or Orla's *anything*—Avner cast a glance toward room 204 and internally cursed himself for the twinge of compassion he felt. If a girl really was crying in there, Avner felt a moral obligation to do *something*.

It wasn't his business, he reminded himself, and the girl—a primary, since this was a primary-only floor—would probably be mortified if he walked in on her sobbing.

"The last thing I wanna do is enter a room alone with you," Avner said as coldly as he could.

"But we wouldn't be alone—the crying girl's in there. And if you don't come with me, I'll probably go by myself and make her feel even worse."

Avner was aware that Orla was coercing him to enter the room with her. Whatever motives she had for convincing him to join her in this benevolent quest were a mystery, but Avner knew he would guiltily dwell on this for the rest of the evening if he didn't at least attempt to help.

"Fine," he acquiesced, refusing to meet her gaze. Pushing past her arm, he stalked into room 204, prepared to encounter a blubbering girl.

There was, in fact, no one in room 204; there was barely

any evidence that anyone dwelled in this dormitory. Both beds were made, though slightly rumpled, and the walls were unadorned except for a small George Washington poster with hearts drawn on it.

After peeking into the bathroom and finding it empty, as well, Avner spun on his heel to stalk toward the exit and reprimand Orla in the hallway. She had already entered the room, though—and closed the door.

"I guess I should have seen this coming," he sighed, running a hand through his hair in aggravation. A grin unfurled on her glossed lips. "Let's not do this, Orla."

"But why not?" She prowled toward him with graceful steps. Avner stood perfectly still, watching her warily as he contemplated an escape route. He had the ability to electrocute her and run, but that felt petty. Then he remembered the bathroom at his back, which connected to the adjacent dormitory.

He began to turn when his body froze, paralyzed by Orla's grip on his t-shirt. Her sharp fingernails dug into his chest, and he shouldn't have liked it, but a horrible, sub-conscious part of him was drawn to her.

"Why not, Av?" she prompted, her face growing steadily nearer to his. Her scent should have repulsed him—anyone's scent other than Zeela's should have—but he felt himself leaning in her direction.

"I-I'm dating Zeela," he insisted, but his body didn't back away.

"So? You've hardly known that blind freak for a year. You've known *me* since we were kids. Remember when we were friends, Av?"

"I—do," he said thickly, straining to swallow. "It didn't last long after you forced me to kiss you."

"Forced? Oh, that's cute. You think you didn't want it? You had a *crush* on me. You admitted it to my face."

"Yeah, but we were *ten*. I didn't want—I just wanted us to be…innocent ten-year-olds."

Orla snorted before unexpectedly bringing one of her nails to his throat. Slowly, she dragged her finger over the sensitive skin of his neck, and heat surfaced within him, involuntarily. "You were never *innocent*. Remember when you electrocuted that boy and he was in the hospital for a month? Remember when you caused a town-wide power outage that killed that poor old woman who stumbled down the stairs—"

"*Stop*," he commanded, but her hands crept beneath his shirt, and he wasn't sure he really wanted her to stop. The worst part was he couldn't tell if she was using her Affinity or if he actually *wanted* her.

At the age of eight, Orla was the first girl Avner had ever interacted with other than Adara. She was kind to him; she understood him and his shameful hatred of his absent parents. It wasn't until she kissed him when he told her not to that he started to realize what she was. Still, he let her cling to him, and he almost *enjoyed* being in her possession until he asked her to tell Kiki to stop bullying Adara and she declined.

His sense of duty to his sister had won then, as his sense of duty to Zeela won now.

"Stop," he repeated, not desperately but definitively. Wrenching himself away, he pivoted toward the door, but she grabbed his chin, forcing him to face her once again.

In his agitation, he forgot not to look directly into her eyes. The moment he did, any sense of free-will evaded him, his thoughts swarming only with Orla. Everything outside this room was inconsequential; he couldn't remember his own name.

"Avner," she breathed, and he was vaguely aware that was him. His eyes drooped when she laced her fingers in his hair. "I liked your hair better when it was black, but...you'll do as you are. I've always wanted you, from the moment you entered our elementary school as an awkward little boy—I told myself I'd marry you. That dream's proven exhausting. You're *difficult*, you know. The most difficult person I've ever had to captivate. If I had to do this every day, I'd be a mess. But for one night, or even just one hour, I can maintain it. Will you make my dreams come true?"

"Yes," his mouth said.

"Good." She pushed him onto the nearest bed, and he fell blissfully into the softness of the sheets, his body thrumming with anticipation as she climbed on top of him. There was a strange sensation brewing in his stomach, as if something about this was inherently wrong, but he couldn't discern what it was.

"I would have been disappointed if you'd said no," she whispered, her breath hot on his skin as she trailed kisses up his jaw. "After all, how am I supposed to impose my revenge on Nero if I don't sleep with you."

Avner's placidity wavered with that. The question was on his tongue—*What are you talking about?*—but he found himself unable to ask it.

"You want me to explain, don't you?" Her smile was feral as she loomed above him, hair cascading around her like a golden waterfall. "Nero thinks himself above me. Just this morning he tried to *kill* me. He thinks we're allies and lovers—and we *were*, for a short day, but I've found that I prefer to work alone.

"So, while Nero thinks I'm convincing you to host another JAMZ session tonight, where he'll redeem himself by beating you and asserting his dominance, I'm really seducing you. Oh, how he'll rage when he discovers his rival, Avner Stromer, had sex with *his girl*. I wouldn't be surprised if he chose to take it out on Mensen. I hope he does."

Mensen. That name rattled his brain, but he couldn't think clearly. Everything was muffled in his mind, a jumble of confusion and desire.

"And when he *does*," she continued, "I'll make sure Fraco's there to witness it. Nero won't survive two offenses within a twenty-four hour period. Periculy will expel him, and with Zeela hopefully dead, you and I will rule this place together, as it should have been from the start."

Zeela. He knew her—she was his…his…

Orla's lips pressed against his ear before trickling back toward his mouth. The physical touch eradicated his swarming conclusions until he couldn't even remember what schemes she'd explained to him.

Unwillingly willing, Avner succumbed to a fraction of Orla's twisted dreams.

Unlike juvie's cafeteria, Periculand's had an unlimited buffet at every meal. Still, Nero didn't hesitate to steal food from others, if only to amuse himself with their flabbergasted reactions. Adrenalized after his morning of planning with Orla, he spent that entire evening at dinner mooching off plates, and upon leaving the cafeteria, he was thoroughly satisfied with his full belly and his display of dominance.

He entered the Residence Tower to the sight of students reading books, watching television, and playing card games, but his attention immediately flew to Orla waltzing down the staircase. Nothing about her had altered from this morning; everything about her was perfectly in place. She simpered at him.

"Did you talk to Stromer?" he asked once they were close enough to speak in hushed tones.

Her eyes twinkled like a vat of gold. "Oh, did I. He's agreed to host another JAMZ tonight. You're still banned, of course, but that'll only work in our favor. If he's not expecting you, he'll be too surprised to react when you demolish him."

"Good," he huffed, as if he'd made the plan and she'd enacted it on his behalf. In reality, Orla had been the one to contrive this scheme, but he didn't want to consider how smart she truly was. It made her seem uncomfortably dangerous. "See you then."

"See you then," she parroted, jumping her eyebrows before she departed the lounge.

Ascending the steps, Nero mentally ran through a sequence of warm up exercises he planned to practice in his dormitory. He landed on the second floor and was headed for room 206 when a small but firm hand grabbed his arm, dragging him across the corridor. Before he'd even caught a glimpse of the person, he stumbled through the door of room 204, which slammed shut behind him.

Disoriented, he searched the room for the perpetrator, but there was no one. The only object with personality was the poster of an old man hanging above one bed. Nero had no idea who the guy was, but he looked ancient, so he concluded this must have been history-freak Jia's room.

"Nero," a hoarse voice hissed. He whipped toward the source and saw nothing. "You're looking at me, but you can't see me. I'm not very good at turning this off…"

Nero's eyebrows screwed in disconcertion, but then he remembered in the van Jerry had sensed a girl none of them could see. "*Blaire*—invisible girl?"

A moment of silence passed before she hiccuped, "Oh, yeah—sorry. I nodded, but you can't see me."

"Why the hell am I locked in your room?"

"Oh—you're not locked in here. I just shut the door so no one would hear us."

"*Why?*" Nero demanded, feeling like he was talking to a door.

She made a strange little coughing noise. "I...overheard something I thought might interest you—and...*witnessed* something."

Nero glanced around the room, suddenly suspicious. Until now, he'd been too consumed by Blaire's strangeness to inhale his surroundings, but he noticed one of the beds was seriously unkempt, and there was a particular scent in the air, like...milk and honey.

"*Tell me,*" he growled, wishing he could see her so he could grab her in a physical threat. Apparently, that wasn't necessary, because Blaire instantly spewed an explanation.

"Well, I was just hanging out in here with the door open when Avner Stromer came in. I was tempted to run, but then Orla Belven strolled in after him and shut the door. It turned, um, sexual pretty fast, and I was too paralyzed with shock to do anything. They"—she gagged—"had sex on my *bed*. Orla told Avner she was doing it to get back at you for almost killing her—"

"And Stromer did it to assert his authority over me," Nero snarled, his breaths now heaving violently. Throughout her story, his hands had curled into fists. In his mind he saw Avner's triumphant face, heard Orla's smug voice—*Oh, did I.*

"Well, actually, no—"

"They're gonna pay," he vowed, red flashing in his vision. "Everyone's gonna pay. This never would have happened in juvie. I was powerful there—respected. It's about time I show this school how the hierarchy really works."

"But, um, Nero—"

"I appreciate your help," he said, not hearing her in the slightest. "It seems at least one person knows their place. You've won a spot as my spy—as long as I have your loyalty, you have my protection."

"Oh. That's... Do I have to watch people have sex again, or..."

"If the need arises," Nero confirmed. The invisible girl emitted a wilting cry, which he ignored. "We have work to do. I have more targets to eliminate than I thought. Come with me."

Swinging the door open, he glanced over his shoulder for her, and seeing nothing, he snapped, "Are you coming?"

"Oh, yes, I'm right behind you," she said, and some part of her invisible body tapped him on the shoulder. It was probably her finger, but it still made him shudder.

"You freak the shit out of me, just so we're clear."

"I'm always clear," she joked with a laugh.

Nero's lips curled in distaste. "You're lucky you're useful. Now, here's the plan: We're gonna scour this town until we find Stromer, Orla, Blind Bitch, Frost-Ass—"

"Who's Frost-Ass?"

"Jamad."

"Right," she said, as if she'd known all along.

"And then I'll beat each one until they're nothing more than a heap of blood."

"Considering blood's a liquid, I don't think it's accurate to call it a *heap*. Also, we should probably do something that's more of a concrete *plan* than just…killing everyone."

"There's nothing wrong with my plan."

"There are a lot of things wrong with your plan," a familiar voice interjected, and as expected, Jerry sauntered up the staircase at the center of the hall. Nero hadn't encountered him since the JAMZ session, but he was too overloaded with vengeance to feel any sort of embarrassment for having clobbered the mind reader's lover.

"For one," Jerry continued, "it's exactly what Orla wants."

"Orla wants to *die*? Well, that's good news. Seems our dreams still coincide."

"She wants you to engage in public violence that'll get you expelled. Which is fortunate for *her*, since your first instinct is violence." Pausing, Jerry surveyed him with his mostly pink eyes, then glanced briefly in the direction where Nero assumed Blaire stood. "From what I've gathered, Orla knew Blaire was in the room while she was with Avner. She knew Blaire would tell you, and she knew you would retaliate with violence. Her plan is to ensure Fraco witnesses that violence and sends you back to prison."

"So, what, I do nothing?" Nero questioned impatiently.

"No, you do whatever the hell you want to do—in secret." Jerry's eyebrows arched mildly, but Nero shook his head.

"How am I supposed to assert myself in this school if no one knows what the hell I'm capable of?"

"Oh, they'll know. They'll all hear about it—even Fraco—but he won't be able to do a damn thing about it because all the witnesses will be too afraid to tattle."

Nero studied him for a skeptical moment. Then his lips widened into a smirk. "Explain."

Remorse coursed through Avner's heart with a higher voltage than any surge of electricity he'd ever produced.

Every step from the second floor to the fifth had felt like an eternity, but even so, Avner wasn't prepared to confront Zeela. He'd spent at least thirty minutes pacing within his own dormitory, mapping out some sort of adequate apology, before he finally forced himself up to the sixth floor.

Luckily, Jamad hadn't been around to witness his distress. Avner dreaded telling his friend about this equally as much; his crush on Orla had been blatant from their first day in Periculand. Plus, Zeela was Jamad's oldest friend, and he was wildly protective of her. Even if it'd never been explicitly stated, Avner knew his roommate would choose Zeela over him in any fight.

And he anticipated this would turn into a fight. Zeela wasn't quick to anger, but Orla had always been a point of contention between them, and Avner had always used the fact that he'd never slept with Orla as proof that he wasn't secretly in love with her. That argument was now dead.

The worst part was that he wasn't sure if he'd be able to stay Zeela's boyfriend, even if she fully forgave him. His guilt would hang between them forever, because even if he hadn't willingly consented, a horrible part of him had *enjoyed* it, and he would never know if it was because of Orla's Affinity or because the boy in him still had a crush on her.

When he arrived on the sixth floor, Maddy stood in the hall, opening the door to room 605. At the sound of his footsteps, she rotated to face him and smiled.

"Hey, have you seen Z?" she asked, peeking into her dark, empty dormitory.

"No..." Slowly, he followed her into the room. "Have you?"

"No, she left dinner a while ago." Maddy sounded unconcerned as she turned on the lights and padded to her side of the room, but Avner's stomach churned with unease. Had Zeela gone looking for him? Had she somehow *heard* of what happened? Avner didn't doubt Orla would hold this information against him, which was why he'd hoped to tell Zeela first.

His gaze wandered to his girlfriend's desk, where her books and papers were abnormally disarranged. When he approached it, he found a crumpled piece of paper atop the chaotic mess. The handwriting was too thick and jagged to be hers.

"Maybe she's in the library?" Maddy offered as she settled into her own desk's chair to work on homework. "I still don't understand how she can read with those eyes, but she does love... Are you okay?"

Avner tore his widened eyes away from the paper to face her. "Yeah...I just...bathroom," he finally blurted out, stuffing the note into his pocket.

"I didn't need to know *that*, but...okay. Good luck," Maddy said, perplexed, as Avner hurried from her room.

He headed for the staircase and almost ran up it until he remembered the damn note. Any guilt he had felt morphed into rage and panic upon reading those sloppily written words:

Stromer—Room 2008. Alone. And shave your head before you come.

8

Allies and Enemies

After dragging Dave, Jia, Haldor, *and* Mensen all the way up to the twentieth floor of the Residence Tower, Nero had to admit that for the first time in a long time he was just a *little* tired. Not fatigued, though; the climb had only been the warm-up.

"Explain to me why I'm here," Jia droned, purple eyebrows raised dully.

The dormitories on the twentieth floor—the highest floor—were vacant and therefore used for storage, so Nero had been able to acquire some rope, with which he'd strapped Jia and Haldor to either of room 2008's swivel chairs. Boulder-boy seemed annoyed but not enough to speak, whereas the history-freak was extremely vocal about her displeasure.

"I could be reading in the library right now," she continued with an aura of self-importance. "I had a date with Thomas Edison!"

"I don't know who the hell Thomas Edison is, but he can wait," Nero retorted, resisting the temptation to shove her swivel chair out the window—with her tied to it, of course.

"By the Bill of Rights!" she blurted out like it was some vulgar swear. "You don't know who *Thomas Edison* is? Juvie really did deprive you of one of the hunkiest inventors in all of—"

"Shut up," he snapped, cracking his knuckles. "Or else."

"Or else *what?* You'll give me a heart attack by telling me you don't know of my other historical crushes, like Frederick Douglass and—"

"Or else," Nero interjected as calmly as he could, "I'll destroy *this*."

From his pocket, he whipped out a poster of some ugly ancient guy, which he'd ripped off her wall. Jia gasped dramatically, attempting to wrench free of her ropes.

"Don't you—that's the only poster of George I brought with me! They don't sell any in Periculand!"

"Then behave," he commanded, spreading his lips into a tight smile.

"I don't see why *you're* complaining," Dave chimed in. "Look at *me*."

Nero's grin widened when he took a glance at the kid hanging upside-down, feet tied to the lighting fixture on the ceiling. Beneath his head rested a large bucket, pooling with the clear acid that dripped from Dave's greenish hair. Only an inch had accumulated so far. Nero wished he could squeeze more out of him.

"You should feel proud, Byle; you're the most important part of this plan—and the least expendable, for now."

"What the hell did I do to you?" Dave grunted, tugging at the ropes that bound his hands behind his back.

"You burned me." Nero inclined his head to display the hair still struggling to grow back. "So now I'm gonna use you to burn my enemies."

"And what did *I* do to become your enemy?" Zeela questioned flatly. She sat on one of the beds, her wrists and ankles constricted with rope.

Nero avoided her freaky eyes and wished he'd grabbed her sunglasses when he'd kidnapped her from her dorm room. "You'll see soon enough."

"Okay, now, I don't want you to freak out and kill George, but I still don't understand why *I'm* here," Jia whined, her voice grating on his ears.

"You're here," he began, jabbing a finger in her face, "so I can determine if you're on my side or if I should dispose of you."

"Why would I *want* to be on your side after you've threatened me and my boyfriends?"

"Dead boyfriends," Dave coughed.

Leaning forward, Nero clutched the arms of her swivel chair and breathed in her face until she outwardly cringed. "You're a history nerd. You know what happens to the losing side of a war. You know the *good guys* don't always win, and you know that *good* is an opinion."

Jia pursed her lips, eyes dark as plums with their severity. "Do you think you're good?"

"To my enemies? Hell no. To my allies? Of course."

"What do we have to do to be your allies?" Haldor huffed in his gravelly voice.

"Fight for me—willingly."

Intrigue altered Jia's features. "Does that mean you'll return George to me?"

"What kind of leader would I be if I didn't?" Nero raised his eyebrows, forcing a display of benevolence. "As my allies, you'll receive all you want and more. We'll rule this school, and all who challenge us will be quenched. Starting with Mensen and Stromer."

"To be clear, I don't have any qualms with you personally,"

Jia said, glancing toward Zeela, "but if Nero can get me some more posters of George—and maybe a few of Abe Lincoln—I can't refuse."

Nero gritted his teeth and wondered if he *really* needed this girl as his ally. She was powerful, but was it worth the weirdness? "Obviously I'll tear apart the town to find these posters."

A swooning smile consumed her lips. "My *hero*! I'm in. Hal, you in?"

"Yeah. Nero's strong."

"Assholes!" Dave barked before physically spitting at them. Jia's face contorted with disgust when the mucus hit her cargo pants. Then she yelped when it burned a hole in the fabric.

"You can spit acid?" she shrieked, shaking her bound legs as if that might save her skin from burning.

"I can spit acid," Dave confirmed, but his eyes widened as if he'd just realized it. "I can spit acid." Then those bulging eyes narrowed as his mouth split into a smirk directed at Nero. "Should've gagged me, idiot."

"Whoa!" The sudden exclamation yanked their attention toward the open doorway, where Avner Stromer leaned against the door frame, panting. "What is going on—and why did you have to pick the highest…"

His words trailed off when his pukey eyes landed on his girlfriend, tethered to the bed like a prisoner. Nero's mood spiked with fiendish delight.

"Welcome, Stromer. You're just in time for the fun to begin."

"I have a feeling your hair is gone but I'm not sure why," Zeela noted, brow crinkling as she studied her boyfriend. Where there had once been locks of black, brown, and neon yellow, there was now a bald scalp, slightly paler than the tan skin of his face.

"I'm not really sure why, either." Avner fixed Nero with an impatient look. "Was the head-shaving really a necessary condition?"

"Oh, it was *wholly* necessary. I might've actually started to pity you if I had to stare at your ugly hair throughout this ordeal."

"Don't listen to his juvenile insults," Dave said to Avner between intervals of spitting toward Nero's feet. His terrible aim would soon burn a hole in the floor. Moaning, the boy wiggled like a suspended worm. "If we fight together, we can beat him!"

"How optimistic of you, Byle." Nero eyed the acid-spit at his feet with distaste. "You're aligning yourself with the losing side, though. I have leverage over Stromer—lots of leverage."

Avner's jaw clenched. "What do you want, Nero?"

"For you to suffer, mostly—but first I should show Dave his place. So, before we get into semantics, why don't you give Byle a little jolt?"

Avner blinked. "A little jolt?"

"Electrocute him."

With a pathetically apologetic expression, he looked at Zeela, as if Nero had asked him to electrocute her and not some helpless kid. Nero should have forced him to zap his girlfriend, but he knew that was the one thing Stromer would rather die than do.

"Should I make the threats first, or are the implications enough?"

"Hold up." Dave halted his squirming to gape at Nero. "You want him to electrocute me? I'm already hanging upside-down! Blood is rushing to my head—my brain will probably explode!"

"Then it's fortunate we're so high in the tower, where no one will hear."

"Nero…" Avner began, like a friend reasoning with a friend.

"Are you trying to *plead* with me, Stromer? I'll start enacting my threats before I even make—"

"No, I don't…want that," he interrupted, defeated.

"Good. Then proceed."

Reluctantly, Avner lifted one hand and ejected a surge of electricity Nero barely saw. A shriek escaped Dave's throat, but he hardly convulsed. The voltage Avner had used on him was far less than what he'd used on Nero—twice.

"Let's try that again, Stromer. More intensity." He wasn't sure any amount of intensity would truly satiate him, though. As long as Dave defied him, Nero wouldn't be pleased. "Unless…"

A tinge of hope lit Avner's eyes. "Unless?"

"Unless Dave swears allegiance to me." Nero spun to face the kid directly. "I shouldn't even bother to offer since you're such an ungrateful prick, but you are my roommate, and I don't like sleeping in the same room as my enemies."

"Yes," Dave said, still panting from the electric shock. "I'll…be your ally."

Nero's eyes slivered as he surveyed the boy's withered pose. "That was too easy. Stromer, again."

"What—no!" Dave begged while Avner winced. Still, Stromer's hand elevated, and he was actually going to heed the command when a delicate hand shoved him to the side.

"Didn't even wait for us to start the show?" Jerry asked as he strolled into the room, guiding Orla by the arm, leaving enough berth for another person—Blaire. Nero knew the mind reader wasn't perturbed that they'd started without him; that had been the plan, after all, and he'd arrived right on time.

"Jerry, glad to see you," Nero greeted with a lazy smile. "Blaire, glad to know you're here. And our guest of honor, Orla."

Clearly, Jerry hadn't hurt her in any way. As when Nero had passed her in the corridor—when she'd acted like she hadn't just banged Avner Stromer—her hair was styled in flawless curls, and her unblemished makeup accentuated all of her appealing features. Her lips pouted and trembled, though, and her shoulders caved inward as if she'd been beaten. Nero almost wished she had.

At the same time, this was the girl he'd opened his heart to, if only for a few days. He never should have trusted her, but a weak, childish part of him craved a companion, someone he could love and care for. Since going to juvie and earning his mother's resentment, he hadn't felt like he could connect with anyone at a sentimental level, and he wanted that, at least with one person.

As proven, Orla was not that person.

"What are you doing, Nero?" she asked, voice quavering.

"Exactly what you wanted me to do," he replied with all the coldness he felt. "Not in the *way* you wanted me to do it, I know, but I outsmarted you, Belven—with the help of my allies, of course. Because I *have* supporters, and you have none."

Her eyes flitted around at the primaries, most of whom were tied like hostages. "This is—*wrong*."

"Save the whining for your turn, Belven. We're still torturing Dave right now."

"I said I would be your ally!" he shouted, writhing and

swaying, acid still dripping from his hair.

Nero turned to Avner, planning to order another jolt, until he found Jerry glaring at him. *Don't go so far that he'll retract an alliance.*

Scowling, Nero ignored him mentally and aloud said, "Where's Dispus?"

Jerry's voice was strained when he responded. "I couldn't find him."

Which Nero knew meant he didn't *want* to find him. Apparently, in Jerry's opinion, his ex-boyfriend had experienced enough super-strength-fueled wrath.

"Unfortunate," Nero drawled, casting a glance in Dave's direction. "I was hoping to knock out all my opponents at once. Plus, I know Byle likes that kid."

"I...don't," the acid-spitter said, sounding as if Nero were physically strangling him. "You're better—more powerful."

"No need to state facts. That's Jia's job in this alliance."

"I'll fill this whole bucket with acid right now if you let me down," he bargained, and it was the first negotiation that actually interested Nero.

"Can he be trusted?" he asked Jerry.

"His offer seems genuine, and I'll know if he starts to think about deflecting." The warning was plain in the mind reader's tone, even though his face remained as impassive as usual.

"All right." Nero yanked Dave's legs, tearing the light from the ceiling and darkening the room to the illumination of a single lamp. Landing headfirst in his own bucket of acid, Dave spluttered and thrashed and kicked until he was on his feet, which Nero untangled from the rope. Once his hands were free, he dutifully began to wring his hair and brush acid off his arms.

"While that's underway..." Nero's gaze wandered back to his enemies. "Stromer, why haven't you properly greeted your lover yet? One jolt should do, but I'd like to see a higher voltage this time."

An inhale, so faint Nero wouldn't have heard it if he hadn't expected it, sounded from behind, and when he glanced over his shoulder, Zeela's face was pinched in revulsion.

"*Lover?*"

Nero chuckled heartily. "Well, I didn't release *that* information correctly—or did I? Any day now, Stromer."

"Zeela..." Avner said, disregarding the demands. "I... It was—"

A fist to the stomach stopped Stromer's stammers— Nero's fist, specifically.

Coughing, the boy straightened from his hunched position, but his expression didn't contain an ounce of defiance—not even self-righteous rage or mild annoyance. Only a bone-deep weariness that implied he would take Nero's punches all night.

"Damn, I forgot—you don't care about your own safety." Marching across the room, Nero hoisted Zeela off the bed by her white hair and dragged her to the bucket. Dave had nearly finished filling it by now, and with one quick move, Nero could have easily dunked the girl's head. "I think it's about time we truly blind your girlfriend—physically, I mean. Emotionally, I'm about to bring her clarity. Did you know, Mensen, that your virtuous boyfriend is a cheater?"

"Nero," Orla interjected sternly.

"Oh, do you want to do the revealing, Belven? This was your mastermind plan, after all: sleep with Stromer, piss me off, get me sent back to jail—I know it all. I'm just informing the public. Although, I'm still unsure about Stromer's motives in all this. I guess he was just a little horny."

"I didn't—it wasn't my idea," Avner pleaded, but he wasn't trying to convince Nero; his repentant gaze was glued to his girlfriend.

"No," Nero conceded, tightening his grip on Zeela's hair, "but you did it, just like you'll electrocute Orla now. Otherwise, I'll dip your girlfriend's head in the bucket, and she'll die knowing Belven was the last girl you slept with."

"This is like watching history unfold," Jia said, eyes protruding wildly. "I can't decide if I love it or hate it."

"I didn't mean to," Avner repeated, his words directed at Zeela but his tone directed at Nero. "I didn't want to—"

"Cut the bullshit, Stromer. You wanted it—everyone here wants it too because it's part of her Affinity. All *I* want is for you to fry that Affinity out of her. If you do that, your girlfriend will stay alive long enough to break up with you when this is over."

"You don't need to hurt Orla to prove to me that you don't like her, Av," Zeela said, her voice too relaxed for someone who was about to face an acidic fate. "I know you wouldn't have done that purposely."

Avner closed his eyes, warding off the panic forming in his features. When they opened again, the irises that had been murky were suddenly a clear, bright yellow.

Nero tensed, anticipating a shock, but Avner threw his hand toward Orla, as instructed. Knowing his intention, Jerry had already removed himself from her, so the burst of energy struck only her, and she flopped against the wall with a scream.

Unfortunately, it wasn't strong enough to do much other than scare her. Aggravated, Nero opened his mouth to bark another order when a spark of pain laced through his nerves, causing him to drop Zeela completely.

"*Stromer*," he growled as the girl collapsed on her stomach. Before she could scramble upright, he yanked her arm and heaved her across the room. Avner was so dumbfounded by this new course of action that he stayed frozen even when Nero hissed in his face, "*Kneel.*"

"I—"

"*Kneel*," Nero repeated, shoving him to his knees. Avner gawked up at him, petrified. "Now beg."

"Don't…hurt her," he said cautiously, his newly neon eyes darting between Nero and Zeela. "I'm…sorry. If you let us go, we won't bother you again."

Nero snorted and seized the boy's shirt. Without giving the couple a moment to react, he towed them into the corridor and threw them down the spiral staircase. Grunting and yelping, the two toppled over each other, Zeela unable to thwart her fall with her bound limbs and Avner tumbling at too swift a pace to stop. They disappeared into the floor below, and Nero retreated to room 2008, half-satisfied.

"That was me dealing with my enemies," he told his allies, half of whom were still tied to chairs. Dave stared at his acid bucket dejectedly, seemingly disappointed it hadn't been used, while Jerry stood diligently between Orla and the exit. "This is me dealing with those who have betrayed me."

Retrieving an unused coil of rope, Nero stomped toward Dave and grabbed his arms, ignoring the stinging sensation as he wove his wrists through the rope.

"What—I didn't betray you! I filled the bucket!"

"I know," Nero assured, tying the knot to constrict Dave's arms before tossing him onto the bed. Since Jia and Haldor remained bound, he moved to Jerry next, lightly securing his hands with a new rope. Then he and Orla were the only two unbound, standing inches apart.

"It didn't have to be this way," Nero said without a hint of apology. "Just remember that."

Her confusion was obvious, but she fabricated a intransigent look, sticking her nose up in the air. "What way? Us as enemies, you mean? It does have to be this way. You ensured that when you abused me."

"I know what I did," he said quietly, "and I know it was wrong. But you don't know what you do, and you don't know how wrong it is. Is one form of abuse so much worse than the next? Aren't we equally evil, you and I?"

Now, Nero, Jerry's voice echoed through his mind. Stepping away from Orla, Nero slipped his hands behind his back, into the binds he'd constructed for himself. They weren't as tight as they should have been, but they served their purpose.

"Fraco, help!" Nero wailed in the most pitiful voice he could muster. He used Hartman's voice as a reference. "Fraco, please, save us!"

"What—what are you doing?" Orla demanded, glancing frantically toward the open doorway.

"Didn't you wonder where Blaire went?" Nero whispered, allowing his lips to curve slyly.

"She's not here?" Jia hissed, scanning the room for the invisible girl. "I thought she was still here."

"No, she's there," Nero said, nodding toward the doorway as Fraco burst in. Blaire, though invisible, was presumably with him, since her job had been to fetch him. Behind the vice principal stood Aethelred, both men wearing unsettled expressions at the sight of five students restricted with ropes.

"What in the world... Someone explain the meaning of

this!" Fraco shrilled, oil spewing from his head as he whipped it back and forth in alarm. "We just saw Mr. Stromer and Miss Mensen injured in the hall below, and now *this!*"

"Orla kidnapped us and brought us up here," Nero sniveled, cowering against the wall. "She did the same to Avner and Zeela and then threw them out. She extracted that acid from Dave and planned to drown us—"

"He does *not* know what he's talking about," Orla insisted, shaking her head.

"What Nero said is true," Jerry said, monotone. "I've never encountered a mind so unhinged."

"Y-yeah," Dave chimed in from his perch on the bed. "She tortured me for my acid."

"Fraco," Orla implored, "you know they're—"

"Call me *Mr. Leve!* Or, frankly, don't call me anything at all! I am repulsed!"

"It must take a lot to repulse you," Jia reckoned. "I'm impressed, Belven."

"I didn't—it wasn't—"

"Mr. Certior, apprehend her this instant! We need to have a word with Mr. Periculy about this outrageous display of insanity. And, you, invisible girl, untie your friends." With a scoff and a squeak, Fraco twirled on his heel and scurried to the stairs. Aethelred gingerly placed a hand on Orla's shirt, tugging on the fabric until, with a high-pitched groan, she acquiesced.

Shrugging out of his loose binds, Nero went around with Blaire to free the others until all six stood together, liberated and giddy. That was how Nero felt, at least. There was still a slight wariness about the others, a faint anxiety that they had not yet escaped all calamity.

It was smart of them to be in awe of Nero's wit—the wit

that had been inspired entirely by Jerry. Nero had always been a predictable barbarian, but now he had proven to possess a cunning mind and the will to destroy his targets.

The alliance between them might have been forced, but it would not fray, because now they knew the moment they betrayed Nero would consequently be the moment of their demise.

Bonus Scene

Through New Eyes

"I simply cannot believe a student would hold other students hostage!" The shrill voice punctured Zeela's awareness, dragging her from the groggy state the fall had thrown her into. Dimly, she was aware that she and Avner were tangled together, probably on the nineteenth floor, and her hands were still bound behind her back. "It is preposterous!"

"I have no doubt there are students in Periculand who are capable of such preposterousness," a more soothing voice countered, one Zeela knew belonged to Aethelred. It echoed from below, along with the sound of hurried footsteps. When her eyes finally squinted open, she looked through the floor and saw Fraco, Aethelred, and a strange, near-translucent figure trekking up the spiral staircase.

"We're listening to a disembodied voice, Mr. Certior! There is nothing about this that is not preposterous!"

"I do have a body," a girl's voice said, "and I'd touch you to prove it, but I don't want my hands to get all greasy."

A gurgle of offense emitted from Fraco's lips, but the girl was spared a snippy reply since they'd arrived on the nineteenth floor, where the vice principal noticed the two fallen teens. "What—what is going on here!"

Avner shifted against Zeela, his brow creased. "Up... stairs," was all he managed to say as he pointed upward. Gaping, Fraco was slow to heed his words, but Aethelred ushered him along, exuding a pale pink aura of sympathy.

"Z, are you okay?" Avner grunted as he disentangled their legs. Since she didn't move or speak, he grabbed her shoulders and propped her into a sitting position. Looking into his face was agonizing, so she focused on her pain, focused on the rope around her wrists and how she would wiggle free of it.

"Here, I'll help you." He hoisted her to her feet, unintentionally inducing aches in her bruised body. Nero hadn't hit her, but the fall down the stairs had done some damage. Still, she bit her tongue, refusing to display her physical discomfort, lest Avner try to comfort her. She did not want his comfort, not after what Nero had revealed.

"Let's hide in one of these rooms," he suggested, guiding them across the hall to the door marked 1902. From above, the vibrations of Fraco's shrieking reverberated, but once they were within the dormitory, Avner shut the door to tune it out.

"I really don't want to deal with an interrogation from Fraco when they come back down," he said, rubbing his neck. "I'd love to see Nero burn in hell, but I think he's made it clear he'll make our lives hell if we..."

Trailing off, he seemed to realize Zeela was still tied up. As soon as he did, he dashed over and toyed with the ropes at her wrists, rapidly but gently. Pain laced up her arms, but she ignored it, refusing to let as little as a breath out until he'd finished.

"Do you wanna...sit down?" he offered, motioning toward one of the two beds as he discarded the rope on the other.

"Not really," Zeela said as she massaged her wrists.

"Do you wanna talk about this?"

His tone was riddled with concern, as was his light blue aura, but the thought of talking about what he'd done brought a sting to her throat. "Not really."

"Do you wanna...break up with me?" he asked, practically suffocating on the words. Since they'd officially started dating last spring, they'd never considered separating, and Zeela hated that they were now.

"A little." Sighing, she slumped onto the bed and met his eyes. "But not really."

Soft yellow washed over him, a sign of relief. He paced toward her and delicately placed himself on the bed at her side, careful to avoid contact. Coyly, he glanced her way and said, "Z, I'm so—"

"No—I just...I know you're sorry, okay, Av? I know you feel guilty, but I don't know how I feel, so I want to sort it out." With a deep inhale, she stared at the rope Nero had used to capture her and continued. "Since we met last year, things have been really great. I love our group—you, me, Maddy, J... I love it."

"But...you don't love me," Avner said carefully.

"No...I do," she admitted with as much hesitation. "And that's why this hurts so much. I knew as soon as I saw you last August that you had feelings for Orla. It was one of the reasons I was leery about letting myself be attracted to you."

"I don't—I don't care about Orla. We have history, but it's over. It was over even before I met you. She's hot, yeah, but only physically, and I've never even wanted her like that. *You're* the only person I've ever wanted. Orla..." His nose twitched as he wrestled with his next confession. "She kissed me when we were young, but I hated it. Every time I kiss you,

I love it. I love *you*—everything about you. I would kill Orla if I thought it would make you happy."

Zeela glared at him from the corner of her eyes, fighting to stifle the smile growing on her lips. "No, you wouldn't."

"I would. I would kill anyone for you," he said, sending a chill up her spine. Avner had never condoned violence—had always been an advocate for peace—but there was no hint of deception in his aura or his voice. "I've never cared about anyone as much as you, and I never will. I won't guilt you into staying with me—I wouldn't want that—and if this is going to be a constant rift between us, maybe we're better off apart, but I'll never stop wanting you."

"Avner," she began, placing a hand on his, "I know you're genuine. I know you wouldn't have slept with Orla on purpose, nor to hurt me. That doesn't mean it won't bother me, but…that's my problem. I'll learn to move past it. You came for me—you shaved your freaking head for me," she added, earning a chuckle from him. "I have no doubt you care for me."

"I guess this was worth it, then," he said, running a hand over his head.

She scrunched her nose. "You're lucky I'm blind. At least Orla probably won't try to seduce you anymore."

"Z—"

"I'm kidding, Av. I'm not so stuffy that I can't joke about it. We've never faced anything his bad, no, but I'd be stupid to think we won't face worse. Every relationship has problems, and if this is ours, then I'm okay with it. Splitting up won't make it any easier. We'll stick together, okay?"

"You don't have to persuade me," he said, raising his hand to caress her cheek. "I'm so sorry Nero came after you. I never wanted to put you in danger."

"You can buy me some ice cream to make up for it?"

He stood, extending a hand to help her to her feet. "We'll go to Declan's Desserts right now—and we'll stay the hell away from Nero, now and forever."

"You don't have to persuade me," she echoed, though she was certain future interaction with Nero wouldn't be their choice to make.

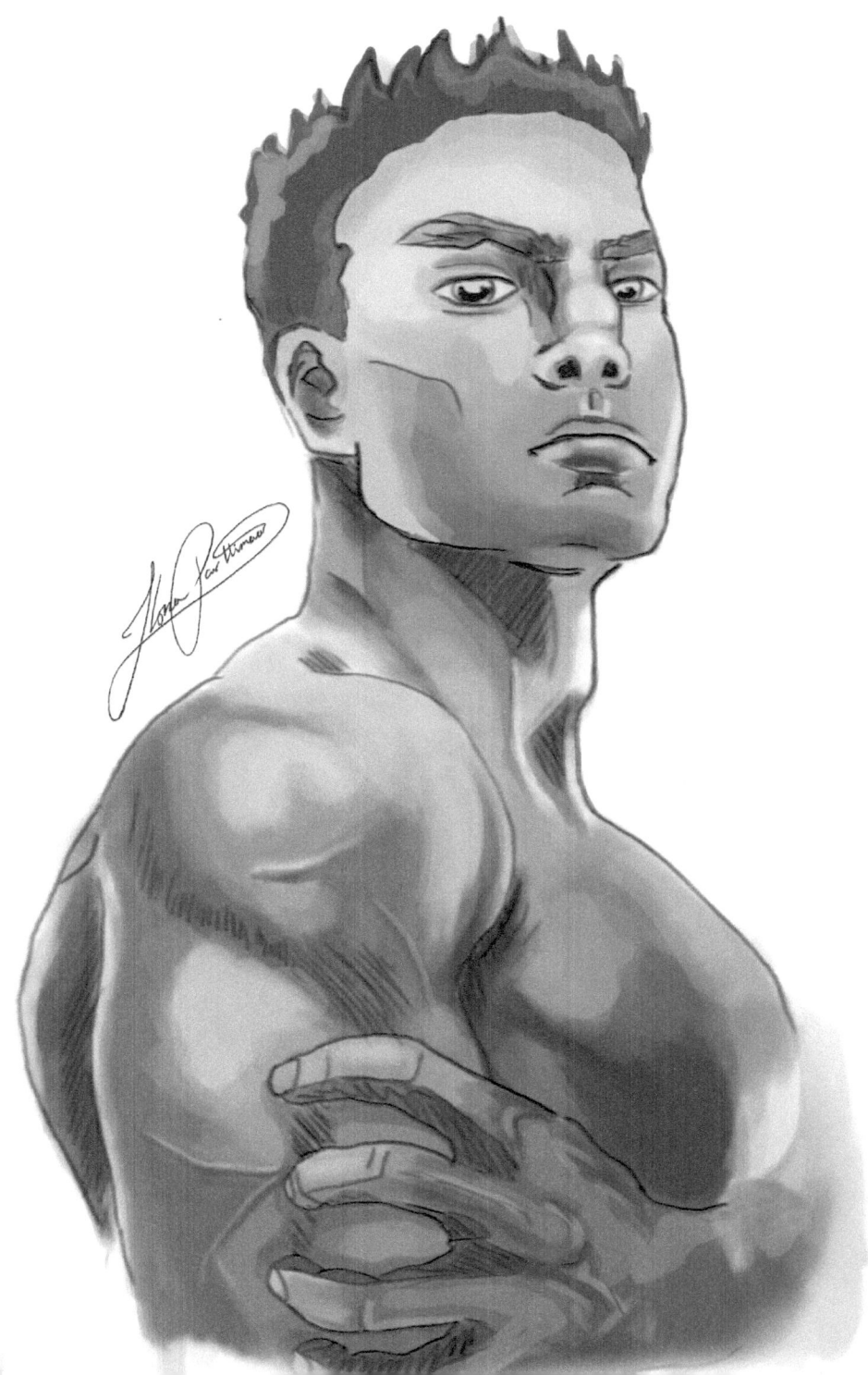

Thank you for reading!

If you enjoyed this novella, please consider leaving a review on Amazon and Goodreads, and make sure to check out the other novels and novellas in The Affinities Series!

www.ingramcontent.com/pod-product-compliance
Lightning Source LLC
Chambersburg PA
CBHW020403130626
46549CB00006B/2421